142 Wellington Place

Jim Selvadurai

Copyright © Tim Selvadurai

All rights reserved. No part of this book may be reproduced in any form or by any electronic or mechanical means, including information storage and retrieval systems, without permission in writing from the publisher, except by reviewers, who may quote brief passages in a review.

ISBN: 978-1-64606-727-5   (Paperback Edition)
ISBN: 978-1-64606-728-2   (Hardcover Edition)
ISBN: 978-1-64606-726-8   (E-book Edition)

Some characters and events in this book are fictitious. Any similarity to real persons, living or dead, is coincidental and not intended by the author.

Book Ordering Information

Phone Number: 347-901-4929 or 347-901-4920
Email: info@globalsummithouse.com
Global Summit House
www.globalsummithouse.com

Printed in the United States of America

Chapter 1

I heard the phone ringing in the hall. I walked towards it from my room and picked it up. Celia seemed very agitated.

"Ben, could you please come over? I've had such awful news. I'd rather not talk about it over the phone. It's about Don."

Don and I had been fighter pilots in the same RAF squadron and had kept our friendship ever since the War ended in 1945, fourteen years ago. My immediate concern was for Don's health.

"Is Don all right? Nothing's happened to him, I hope," I said, my voice rising with anxiety.

"Oh, no," Celia said, a trifle impatiently. "Nothing like that, but please do come as soon as you can. You won't delay, will you?"

"I'll come along right away," I said. "My car has gone to the garage for repairs, so I'll have to take a taxi, but I'll be with you as soon as I can."

"Oh, thank you, Ben," Celia said. "Sorry for being such a bother."

I rang the taxi service, and the receptionist confirmed they would send me a taxi in ten minutes.

It was a Saturday, and I had been looking forward to a restful afternoon and a nap, so Celia's call made me a trifle cross-grained. I chided myself for letting my feelings get the better of me; Celia was not the sort of person to drag me out of my home unless there really was something the matter.

I was also irritated partly because I had already changed into a comfortable pair of silk pyjamas with the intention of settling myself into a chair with a book. Having to answer Celia's summons meant changing again. I undressed hastily and put on my suit, brushed my hair, rigged on my tie, and, with a quick glance at my watch, which read three p.m., sped out of the room. I wondered what could be wrong as I stepped into the taxi.

"Craven Manor," I said, settling myself comfortably into the back seat.

If Don was not ill, then he must have got himself into some kind of trouble. Celia and Don were such a happy couple; they were devoted to each other. I wondered what could have happened to disrupt Celia's usual complacency. Though she had not said exactly what was troubling her so much, I had an uncomfortable suspicion that Don had done something foolish.

The taxi sailed up the drive at Celia's home and jerked to a stop under the porch. I alighted. Before I could ring the bell, Celia opened the door. She was wearing a well-fitting white dress with navy-blue polka dots that accentuated her willowy figure. She had a smooth, ivory complexion, and the black mass of hair that fell softly on her shoulders was arresting.

"Do come in, Ben," she said, her brow puckered with worry. Her rigid body and clenched fists reflected her state of mind. "There's a woman in the hall who says that she's pregnant. She says that Don is the father. She has Don's letters as proof."

For a moment I could say nothing. Though I'd known of Don's dalliances in the past, I couldn't believe that he'd get himself into this sort of mess. He was too devoted to Celia, and he'd changed a lot since his marriage. Before that, Don had been a bachelor for far too long. He had married at the age of thirty-six and had been rather the gay dog until he had met Celia. Being a handsome man with an easy charm, he was a great favourite with the ladies, and his amours had been numerous. He had been very much a man of the world, rather set in his ways, and inclined to be quite vain. His marriage to Celia, however, had so changed him that in the eyes of his friends, his transformation had seemed no small miracle. From being the hard-drinking clubman and bon vivant, he had settled down and become an attentive husband who hardly ever drank and who seemed quite content to spend his evenings at home. At first his friends were sceptical; they knew that

Celia was wholly instrumental in this change, and they joked among themselves that the poor man was confined to quarters against his will. But Don didn't seem in any way restrained; on the contrary, his demeanour conformed in every respect to that of the happy and contented husband.

"Will you see her, Ben?" Celia said. "I just don't know what to say or do, I am so frantic. How could Don have done such a thing? How could he?" She whimpered.

I could not help feeling protective and moved to tenderness at Celia's plight. It was not so long ago that I, too, had loved her. Had Don not come along and swept her off her feet, it was very likely that she would have consented to be my wife. All that was almost four years ago and the ardour of my love had considerably cooled, yet Celia still held a vague fascination for me.

She was not at all pretty in the conventional sense of the word, but she had a lissom body and a softness in her quiet, serious face with its large lambent eyes and well-proportioned mouth, which held a subdued loveliness that was altogether attractive and quite irresistible.

"Where's Don?" I said.

"He's in London at a board meeting with the education authorities. He'll be back only on Tuesday."

"It'll be all right," I said gently. "You'll see. I think I'll go and talk to her now."

I entered the hall and saw its large, open bay windows and the elegant silver sofa set in front of them. An oblong mahogany coffee table and a couple of tall floor lamps with off-white shades which flanked the sofa completed the picture. The woman in the hall was small, about five feet, three inches tall and very trim, with black hair, jet-black eyes, and a clear but pale olive complexion.

I said, "I am a friend of Mr Murray's, and Mrs Murray has asked me over. You may feel free to talk to me."

She was seated forward on the edge of her chair with her knees pressed together and her hands clasped tightly in her lap. She shook all over and looked rather pathetic. Her eyes were wide and glazed.

It was obvious, even before she spoke, that she was a foreigner. Her dark hair and eyes seemed to suggest Spanish descent. She was very attractive in a fragile sort of way. When she did speak, she had a strong accent that was curiously pleasant to the ear.

She told me that she was going to have Don's baby and that she was already two months pregnant. Haltingly, she recounted how she had first met Don at a cafe in London, on Regent Street, called the Black Wolf.

He had seemed very nice, and they had got to talking. He had offered to take her home. After that he had come to see her often. He had said that he was in love with her; she hadn't realised at first that he was married – he had told her so only later. And now that she was going to have his child, she was desperately worried.

"But why did you come here?" I asked. "What could you gain?"

"He hasn't been seeing me for some time now," she barely whispered, her eyes fixed on the floor. "And when I told him that I was carrying his child, he said that it wasn't true and that I was never to see him again."

This was one of those moments when one says nothing because there is nothing one can say. I needed to meet with Don to find out if all this was true, and I was truly at a loss for what to do next – especially what I should say to Celia.

"Miss … er …?"

"Adriana Hamilton," she said.

"Miss Hamilton," I said, "there is nothing that we can do now until we talk to Mr Murray. I will tell him that you called, and I dare say you will hear from him. He isn't likely to be back for a day or two."

She must have understood from the note of finality in my voice that she was being asked to leave. She stood up and picked up her little beaded handbag from the settee. She wiped her eyes clean, and a resoluteness now replaced her wilted, worn-out expression. She gave me the impression that she was trying to be formal and firm, but the attitude didn't quite carry; she still seemed a bit nervous.

"I need £5,000 to pay for the doctor and other expenses." The words came out in an almost incoherent rush, as if it were a line she had memorised and would forget if she didn't speak it all at once. She was flushed and breathless, and she kept her eyes on the floor.

Before I could quite find my tongue, she said, "There is a man in London who will do an abortion for £2,000. I must have it out before it's too late. You can tell Mr Murray that I have his letters." Although her voice sounded thin and weak, there was no missing the threat in her reference to the letters. Until now, I had quite forgotten about them.

"Have you Mr Murray's letters with you now?" I said, and she nodded. She opened her bag and pulled out a thick envelope which contained a number of folded blue papers. She pulled out one of the papers and handed it to me.

I could hardly believe it, but there could be no doubt that it was Don's handwriting. I didn't want to pry, but I felt that it was in Don's interest that I read it.

It began, "My own darling girl" and ended with "Your adoring Don." My eyes scanned the rest of the contents hastily. It was a surprisingly sloppy, sentimental letter, and I found myself wondering how Don could have allowed himself to concoct such mawkish rubbish. It was unabashedly amorous, obviously the writing of a man whose passions had been aroused. Most of it referred to how much he desired her and how much he was looking forward to meeting her again. It made me feel a trifle uncomfortable.

I handed it back to her. She put it into the envelope and shut her bag.

"Tell him," she said, her voice rising in pitch unnaturally, "that if I don't hear from him by Monday I shall expose everything to the Church authorities. I need the money urgently. He knows where to contact me." With what seemed an effort of will, she looked me straight in the eye, and there was a glint in hers that reflected the malice of those words.

"You will hear from him," I said almost compulsively. She stepped hurriedly across the carpet and opened the door.

Chapter 2

Celia was upstairs waiting for me. She had been crying, and she wore an expression of alarm, almost of panic. When she saw me she didn't say anything and started to sob hysterically.

For a long time I said nothing. She sat on the bed, her tall, slender frame convulsing. I felt very sorry for her; I knew that her husband's infidelity was something she could never accept, understand, or bear. Secretly, I detested Don for what he was doing to her. I looked at Celia's face, which, despite her anguish, was so lovely, her flushed skin adding to her Madonna-like beauty, and wondered how Don could have treated her so disgracefully.

"Celia," I said gently, "it's no good crying. Things will turn out all right eventually. You'll see."

I knew how hollow my words were, but under the circumstances, there was hardly anything else I could say.

Celia wiped her eyes and made an effort to stop crying. She raised her head and took a deep breath in an effort to control herself.

"They were Don's letters, weren't they?" she asked.

"I am afraid so," I said wretchedly.

"Do you think he loved her?" she said. "Or was she just a piece of fluff to tickle his vanity? I could never forgive him for that."

"Look here," I said, not wanting her to talk or think too much. "You said that Don was due back on Tuesday, didn't you? Well, that's three days from now. I do think that I'd better go down to London and meet him this evening. I have some business to attend to there and can kill two birds with one stone."

"Yes, I suppose you'd better," she said, and then, as if talking to herself, "I hate him, the beast." Her voice grated and her face contorted in disgust.

I said nothing but put my arm around her shoulder to calm her.

"I am sorry to put you through all this bother," Celia said with an affected smile. "You've been awfully kind, Ben. You must forgive me for my histrionics. You know how hard I've tried to give Don a good home. When I married him – well, you know how he was. Women had rather spoilt him. He was the sort of man as much sinned against as sinning. I thought that my love had changed him, and I was so happy. But to think that all this time it had only been a pretence – such an awful, hideous lie. It's so humiliating. He has no regard for me at all; otherwise, how could he have been so callous as to write to this wretched foreign minx? Such an ordinary slip of a girl, at that."

She sobbed violently again, and I squeezed her shoulder more tightly.

"Celia," I said, "I don't know what came over Don, but I do know that he loves you. I know the whole thing looks ridiculous, but it's no use upsetting yourself, so please try not to cry." I looked at my watch; it was nearly four thirty p.m. "I should try to get to London as early as possible. I really must be going now."

I rose, and Celia wiped her face with the palms of her hands and got up hurriedly. "I am sorry I can't drive you home," she said. "My car won't start. Something's wrong with the ignition. I must get a mechanic to look at it."

"That's okay," I said. "I should have no problem in catching a taxi. Is Mrs Feston in?" I knew it would be very lonely for Celia after what had happened.

"No," Celia said, "she's away for a few days in Croydon visiting her nephew. I wish she were here."

Mrs Feston was Celia's housekeeper – a genial old woman who doted on Celia. Celia's parents had employed her as a nurse when Celia was born.

Celia's father had been bred in India; his family had been in tea planting in Darjeeling. He had no immediate connections in England. He had met Celia's mother whilst in India. She was the youngest daughter of a Welsh doctor attached to one of the tea estates, and after a whirlwind romance, she and Celia's father had married. After Celia's birth, they had decided to settle in England, where they bought the very manor in which Celia now lived, in Wimbledon. Celia was their only child, and they had lavished every kindness upon her. Mrs Feston had, over time, become one of the family, an old retainer. She took over the task of mothering Celia after her mother had died, when Celia was only a girl of twelve. Celia's father had been dead six years by then, and although Celia had been well provided for, as her father had been a man of means, she had no one to turn to but Mrs Feston, who ran a home for her as best as she could here at Craven Manor. When Celia had announced her intention to marry Don, Mrs Feston had protested at first, for she had come to hear of Don's reputation with women, but had later, albeit reluctantly, given her blessing.

"By the way, where is Don putting up in London?" I asked at the door. "Is it the usual place? The Clarendon at Wellington Place off Regent Street?"

"Yes," Celia said, "the Clarendon."

I had visited Don there before on one or two occasions whilst he was in London.

"I'll get in touch with you as soon as I get back. That might be a bit late, though, nine thirty or ten, as I have an engagement with a client."

I waved to Celia as I walked down the drive.

Chapter 3

I felt weary and heavy headed as I walked out of the manor's grim iron gates and stepped onto the road. The evening air was crisp and cool. I drank in a few draughts and realised that under normal circumstances, a walk would have done me a world of good; it was less than a mile and a half to my home. However, there was no time for that now. I stopped the first taxi that went by and directed the driver to my address.

As the taxi turned a corner, the white gates of my residence came into view. It was situated in one of the quieter residential areas on the outskirts of town, a good two or three miles from the main thoroughfare and the shopping district. It was quite definitely the most picturesque residential area in Wimbledon, and the homes belonged to the more wealthy members of the town's populace, one of whom, as good fortune would have it, I happened to be. If the truth must be told, I had been lucky to inherit money. Being an only child, my parents had left all they owned to me. Besides, my good fortune had extended beyond mere property; by virtue of my father's good name and connections, I had inherited a sizable part of his law practice as well. He had been a solicitor for many years, and after his death, it seemed only natural, as I had also qualified as a solicitor, that I should carry on where he left off.

I asked the driver to stop by the gate, paid him, and walked down the drive. I noted that my car had still not come back from the garage. Dusk was setting in, and I could see that Tomlinson, my butler, had already put on the lights in the hall and on the porch. He must have seen me coming, for he had opened the door and was standing beside it. He had not seen me leave, as it had been his afternoon off.

"Good evening, sir," he said. "I saw you come up the drive."

He was in his late seventies, but he was by no means feeble. He was thin and tall and carried himself very straight; he had the gait of a man of sixty. Old Tomlinson had been with the family from the time I was a mere boy, and he was a great asset to me.

"Shall I get you a drink, sir?" he asked in his piping voice. He clearly noticed that I was tired.

"Yes, please. I will be down in a while," I said. "I've got to go to London by the first possible train. Could you call a taxi in half an hour?" I called over my shoulder as I proceeded hastily up the stairs to my room.

I took a shower, packed a few things into a bag, and was about to leave when the phone rang. It was Celia. "Ben," her voice came faintly down the line, "you haven't gone yet, thank goodness. You must promise me something, Ben – please don't tell Don that I know anything about this ... this horrible business. About the woman, I mean."

"But Celia," I said, "what else can I tell him? Surely—"

"Tell him the woman came to your place, and not here, and that you haven't told me a thing yet. Please, will you do as I say? You see, I have an appointment with him on Tuesday afternoon. It was agreed before he left that I should join him for some shopping and accompany him back, and I intend to bring up the matter with him myself then. He wouldn't be able to face me if he knew that I knew about this affair. Don't you see? It would make things easier for both of us if he didn't think I knew."

Perhaps Celia was right. Perhaps it would be best if Celia herself were to speak to him directly about the whole lurid business. After all, it would make it easier for Don to meet Celia if he believed she knew nothing.

"All right," I said reluctantly. I wasn't very comfortable with the prospect of my having to lie to Don when I met him.

"Thank you. Don't forget, he must think I know nothing," Celia said. "And do ring me as soon as you return. I'll be waiting to hear from you."

"Your drink, sir." Tomlinson was standing at my elbow with a tray in his hands.

I gulped down the whisky and soda, thanked Tomlinson, and went to the taxi, which had just parked under the porch.

"I shan't be in for dinner," I said before getting in. "Don't wait up for me. I'll probably be quite late."

Chapter 4

I boarded the train to London a little before six p.m. I chose an empty compartment and sat down in a corner seat by the window.

I got to thinking of my mission, and my mind drifted to the afternoon's events. Everything seemed surreal. Yet there was no mistaking it: those were, beyond any doubt, Don's letters, and there was no mistaking the intimacy of Don's relationship with this woman. Adriana Hamilton – yes, that was her name. What was she up to? I wondered if it could be blackmail. She seemed strangely detached. Although she did seem perturbed, one would have expected greater … er … *sincerity* in her expression of her feelings. Something in her story didn't ring true; there was something coldly deliberate and rehearsed in her attitude, as if she were playing a role. I resigned myself to the cosiness of my seat. I could hardly wait to meet Don and hear what he had to say.

I awoke with a start when the train came to a halt; I had dozed off. I looked out of the window to get my bearings. People were milling up and down the platform, and I could see the words "Waterloo Station" on the platform board. I had woken up just in time. Smoothing my trousers, I alighted from the train, crossed over to the adjoining platform, got into the Underground, and took the Tube to Oxford Circus. Once back on the street, I hailed a taxi to Don's place.

"Where to, sir?" the driver asked.

"142 Wellington Place, off Regent Street," I said. "It's a little hotel called the Clarendon."

It took only ten minutes to get there. I paid the driver and walked up the steps to the door. On the wall just inside was a plaque bearing the names of the tenants. I rang the bell next to Don's name and waited.

Although the place was called a hotel, it wasn't really so. It was like any other rooming house, except that they did serve breakfast. Most of the occupants took their breakfasts down in the basement. It was quite a clean place with a few neatly laid-out dining tables. The walls had been recently painted off-white, giving them a bright and glossy appearance.

The door opened sooner than I expected, and Don's face peeped through. "Hello," he said, grinning broadly. "This is a happy surprise. Come right in."

I entered and Don closed the door.

"You needn't have rung," he said. "The front door's not locked. The lock's been broken for some time now."

We walked down a carpeted corridor, and Don stopped by the first door on the left. We went inside quite a large room, bright and airy. The windows faced the street, and on sunny days, the sunlight coming through would illuminate the entire room. The curtains, now drawn over the windows, were cheery – azure with darker blue checks – further brightening the room. There was a double bed covered with a blue bedspread, a sturdy oak table, and three chairs. The walls had been recently covered with mottled grey-and-blue wallpaper.

A small cubicle to the right of the bed housed the bathroom and toilet, the door of which was ajar.

"Well, this is a surprise," Don repeated in that effusive manner that so became him and gave one the satisfying impression that he was always glad to see you. "I must say, you've brightened my day. I really was feeling rather down in the dumps. Have a cigarette?"

"You know I don't touch the stuff anymore," I said. I had been a heavy cigarette smoker but had given it up more than a year before. I had cultivated the habit of an occasional pipe instead.

"Of course! I'd forgotten," Don said. "But what about a drink? Would you like a scotch? Don't mind if I don't have one, though. A little too early for me."

"No thank you," I said.

I said nothing for a while. I hadn't the heart to bring up the awful news I had come all this way to tell him. He didn't seem to suspect that anything was wrong, and he looked so cheerful and acted so well disposed that my heart sank at the thought.

I found myself sympathising with him. He was really a very good-looking man, and he had an irresistibly pleasant, friendly manner. I looked at his strong, well-moulded face with its straight nose, clear blue eyes, pleasantly chiselled mouth, and full lips, and I wondered whether a man like Don Murray could really be blamed for his frailties and frivolities. Such men seemed to be always running into trouble with the fair sex, quite often in spite of themselves.

Don must have noticed something in my manner, for his face suddenly clouded. "Anything the matter, Ben?" he asked.

I cleared my throat. "Yes, I am afraid so," I said. "Something rather ugly has cropped up—"

"Is Celia all right?" he cut in anxiously. "Nothing wrong with her, I hope."

"No, no she's all right – nothing to do with her. It concerns some woman who says that she is pregnant and that you are responsible," I blurted out, feeling not a little out of my depth.

For a moment Don said nothing. His whole body tensed. It was obvious that this news had had a profound effect on him.

"But how did you get to know about it?" Don said, and then he added with deep anxiety, "Does Celia know?"

"No, she doesn't," I said, looking away so my face would not reveal anything. I then told him what had happened – saying, of course, that the woman had come to see me, leaving Celia completely out of the picture.

"Thank goodness Celia doesn't know," he said. I squirmed. "Ada must have checked your address from the telephone directory," he mused. "She knew that we were friends."

"How did it all happen? I thought you had put all that behind you. This is quite a mess," I said. "And she has your letters. Really, how could you have been such a fool to expose yourself by writing to her?"

Don reached into his trouser pocket and fetched a packet of cigarettes. I watched him light one with shaky fingers. I couldn't help feeling sorry for him.

"It was just one of those things – one of those situations that one finds so difficult to cope with. You know how I had turned over a new leaf after I married Celia, and that wasn't just eyewash, either. She was so wonderful and always managed to bring out the best in me. For four years I stayed away from drinking and women – all the things I had been used to. I never had anything to do with another woman in all those years, although God knows I had plenty of opportunities. And then I met Ada."

Don inhaled deeply off his cigarette and blew out a large puff of smoke. He reached for the ashtray, and his finger kept tapping his cigarette nervously.

"I met her last spring, when I was here on one of my visits, at a pub in Regent Street just up the road. I had gone in for a snack and a pint. She was seated at a table opposite me, alone, sipping a drink. You know how beautiful she is;

I couldn't resist looking at her. It probably wouldn't have gone beyond that, but she smiled at me with those devilish eyes of hers, and I was captivated. I walked across to her table and sat down. I don't know what came over me, but I was drawn to her like a magnet. We got to talking, and presently she invited me to her place. I really fell for her – no one else could have had such an effect on me."

Don took another deep puff off his cigarette and let the smoke stream out of his nostrils. He continued, "Well, anyway, I got to seeing her often, mostly during the lunch interval, and sometimes in the evenings after work, when I would stay out later than usual on the pretext to Celia that I was working late. Occasionally, she would stay nights with me here at the hotel. I didn't visit her flat during the day, of course, except on Saturdays and Sundays if I was in town, since I was busy at the office. One day, however, I thought I'd surprise her. I took a day off and went to pay her a visit. I knew that she didn't have a job – she told me that she was staying in London only for a short holiday and that she would be going back to Malta after a few months. Her mother is Maltese but her father is English – hence her English surname. She told me her father settled down in Malta many years ago. She gave me the impression the family were fairly well off.

"It was one of those bright summer mornings. I had come in my car that morning, and I drove to her place. I thought we could drive somewhere for the day. She lived in a neat little flat in Bayswater behind the Tube station. I parked alongside the pavement and got out. I rang the doorbell and waited, but there was no reply. Disappointed, I got back in the car and drove slowly towards Bayswater Road, and I spied her coming down the road with a man by her side. She didn't see me. I waited until she was a little way off and turned back towards her flat. I parked in an alley not far from her place and waited. The man accompanied her into the flat. I don't know why, but I had a terrible suspicion that something odd was going on. I thought I'd wait awhile longer and observe what was happening before going up and ringing the bell. After about twenty minutes, the door opened and the man walked out alone. I was about to go up to the flat when Ada then came out. She walked towards Queensway, and I followed her. When she reached Bayswater Road, she stopped and stood on the pavement. I watched her for some time, but she didn't move from where she stood. She looked provocatively at the men who passed her. Presently a man came by and spoke to her; they exchanged a few furtive words, and then he walked back with her to the flat. Then it dawned on me. Of course, she was a prostitute."

Don lit another cigarette. His face had a hangdog quality about it.

"Well, to cut a long story short, that ended my relationship with her. I was terribly fond of her, you know, but this was a terrible shock. I couldn't get over the fact that she had been duping me all along. I felt cheated and disgusted. She tried to make up with me, but I was not going to have anything more to do with her. She was very persistent, however, and kept calling me at the office. She seemed desperate.

She said she loved me, that she was sorry, that she would change, and so on. Then one day she rang me up and said that she was pregnant with my child. I didn't believe her, of course; I knew it was a ruse. After all, she'd been around with all kinds of chaps every day. I wasn't going to let her fool me. I told her so and rang off. That was a couple of weeks back, and I haven't heard from her since. I thought it was all over, but now this happens."

I watched Don's face, quite haggard with worry. I wondered how best I could help him, but I knew only too well how deeply in trouble he was. This would disrupt his domestic life, which was terrible in itself, but in Don's case, it would also have far-reaching social and professional consequences. He was on the board of directors of a consortium of Church of England–run schools, and he also acted as an inspector of schools. Should his conduct come to light, the Church authorities would most certainly have little hesitation in calling for his resignation, if not his dismissal.

"Don," I said, "I'm afraid things don't look very bright just now. As long as she has your letters, she has the whip hand over you. She says that she wants £5,000 for an abortion and personal expenses, and she wants a reply by day after tomorrow. I dare say she'll call. She has threatened to expose you to the Church authorities if you don't pay, and I think she jolly well means business. You realise, of course, that this could be the beginning of long-term blackmail."

Don rose and paced the room, his hands stuffed deep into his trouser pockets.

"Well, what can I do?" he said, his voice rising in desperation. "I haven't much choice, have I? I did take away quite a few of my letters to her the last time I saw her. I had a suspicion that she would use them against me, but I couldn't lay my hands on all of them. She must have had a few tucked away out of reach. Oh, I've been a fool, such a fool."

"It does seem ridiculous, but it would seem that there's no way out now but for you to pay."

"You're quite right, of course. But I can't get hold of £5,000, or even much less. I do have a few thousand in the bank, but it's in a joint account with Celia"

I watched Don continue to pace like a caged animal.

"I could lend you the money," I said.

"That's kind of you, but it's no use. I suppose I could spin a yarn to Celia and withdraw the money, but is that going to help? Ada's bound to keep coming back for more. No, paying her isn't the answer." Don lit a cigarette. "There's one thing I'll have to try first, and that's to get in touch with her to see if I can sort things out. I'll give her a call tonight. If that fails, I suppose I'll have to pay," he said.

I knew, of course, that Don's plan to appeal to this woman was just a fantasy; he was obviously deceiving himself into believing that he could win over his former mistress with smooth talk and charm, or whatever other means he intended to use. But I didn't want to contradict him. I only said, "You can try, but remember that as long as she has your letters, you are at her mercy. You've got Celia and your job to consider."

I got up. "Don't delay too long," I said. "She seemed urgently in need of the money, and I think she meant it when she said she would expose you if she didn't receive payment."

"Yes, I suppose you're right. It's so unlike her, though. I wouldn't have thought she'd have come to you directly without telling me first that she needed the money. It is all very puzzling. Anyway, I'll try to call her right away."

I walked to the door, and Don followed me out.

"Thanks, Ben," he said. "I'll let you know how things get on. Celia will be coming over here on Tuesday. She was keen on some shopping. All this is so upsetting, but I reckon it will all sort itself out. Everything should be all right as long as Celia doesn't know."

As I opened the building's main door, a dwarfish man who seemed to be in a great hurry to get in bumped squarely into me, nearly throwing me off balance. He sported a toothbrush moustache and a felt hat. He apologised profusely, and we shook hands.

As I stepped onto the street, I looked at my watch. It was almost 8.00 p.m. I had a dinner appointment with James Falkland, the director of an insurance company who were my clients, at the Cafe Mozart in Park Lane at 8.30. I decided I would have enough time to stroll to the nearest pub and order myself a beer before the meeting. It didn't take me five minutes to get to a pub. I sat at a small table for two in a corner and took my time sipping a Heineken. I dreaded the idea of having to face Celia and confirm the unsavoury truth. And I felt guilty at having had to deceive

Don about Celia's knowledge of the whole affair. My mind wandered to various approaches for best dealing with the messy situation and to various solutions, but none of them were viable. By the time I had finished my beer, it was already eight fifteen. I took a taxi to the Cafe Mozart and arrived five minutes late for my appointment.

Chapter 5

When I reached home, it was around ten forty-five p.m. and I was tired. Tomlinson had left me a note informing me that my car had arrived. I thought it best to have a shower and a change of clothes before going to see Celia. It was depressing that I had nothing cheerful or hopeful to tell her, and meeting her would no doubt be an irksome task, but it had to be done.

When I rang, Celia answered the phone. She seemed tense and breathless, as though she was trying hard to control an upsurge of emotion.

"Is anything the matter, Celia?" I said.

"No, no," she answered. Her voice steadied a bit. "It's nothing. I … I was frightened when I heard the phone ring. It's so late. Please do come over as soon as you can."

"I won't be long," I said. There was no response; the line seemed dead. "Are you there, Celia?" I asked, wondering if she had rung off.

"Yes, yes. I am sorry," she said. "I was listening. Yes, please come over; I shall be waiting."

I rang off and put on my coat. Dodson, my chauffeur, had brought the car in from the garage. It being his day off, I drove myself to Celia's. When I rang the bell, Celia opened the door. Her smile seemed forced, and she was very pale. We went into the sitting room. Celia went over to the liquor cabinet and poured me a whisky and soda. She poured herself one too and came and sat down.

"What happened?" she said. "Did you meet Don?"

She clutched the drink between her hands.

I told her what had happened and also added the woman's request for £5,000, which I had not mentioned to her before. I didn't see any point in keeping this information from her now.

It was difficult to talk to Celia; she was unusually restrained and uncommunicative, as if anything she might say would expose some dark secret. I got the impression that she was no longer interested in anything I had to say.

She said, "Yes. I shall, of course, agree to pay whatever is required."

It was getting late, fifteen minutes past midnight, according to my watch. I rose to leave when the doorbell rang. Celia was startled by the noise. In the capacious stillness of that house, at so late an hour, it did seem rather an eerie sound.

"Are you expecting anyone?" I asked, walking across the hall to answer the door. Celia said she wasn't.

When I opened the door, there were two men outside, both wearing overcoats and felt hats. One of them, a tall man with a stoop, showed me his badge.

"I am Inspector Hargreaves of the Wimbledon Police," he said. "We would like to speak to Mrs Murray." He introduced the man accompanying him as Sergeant Bates.

I introduced myself by name and said that I was a friend of Mrs Murray's.

"Do come in," I said, wondering what could have brought these men. Inspector Hargreaves and his colleague stepped into the hall. On seeing Celia, Hargreaves bowed, and his face took on a solemn expression.

"Mrs Murray?" he queried, and Celia nodded. The Inspector cleared his throat. "We are sorry for barging in at so late an hour. I'm afraid I've got some bad news for you. We have had a call from the London Police that your husband – er … you must prepare yourself for the worst – that your husband was found dead in his room this evening. I am sorry."

Celia put her hands to her face and sat down heavily on the chair by her side. A muffled cry escaped her lips. I couldn't believe my ears. There must have been some mistake.

"But Inspector," I said, incredulous, "surely you are mistaken. It can't be. I saw him this very evening. I've only just returned from visiting him in London. It's impossible."

This seemed to arouse the Inspector's professional interest, as he raised an eyebrow and looked more intently at me. "You saw him this evening?" He hesitated. "In that case, we would like a statement from you later on, Mr Benison, if you would be so kind."

"Yes, of course," I said, still in a daze.

Celia hadn't moved from the chair. Her hands were still cupped over her face, her body shaking with the sobs she tried unsuccessfully to stifle.

I put my arm round her shoulder. "Excuse me, Inspector," I said, "has the cause of death been established?"

"I am afraid so. There was a strong smell of gas in the room, and it is likely that the gas killed him. Anyway, we can't be certain until after the autopsy." The Inspector seemed to be holding something back.

"Are you suggesting that it was suicide?" I asked incredulously.

"We honestly don't know," he said matter-of-factly.

Celia continued to sob silently in the chair. She didn't say a word. She was obviously in shock.

"Could we have a brief statement from you now? You can then come to the station tomorrow," the Inspector said to me.

I recounted the main events of the day, including, inevitably, the account of Miss Hamilton's visit, my mission to talk with Don, and my movements thereafter, until my return to Wimbledon and arrival at Celia's. I didn't see any sense in shielding Don now, and being a solicitor, I had the good sense not to conceal facts from the police.

The Inspector stopped me from time to time with a question.

"You are quite sure, Mr Benison," he said after I had finished, "that you left Wimbledon on the six p.m. train and arrived in London at approximately six forty-five and that your visit to Mr Murray happened approximately between seven and eight? And after that, you visited a pub and went to your appointment around eight thirty, finished your discussions around nine fifteen, took the train at about nine forty-five, and arrived at Wimbledon at approximately ten thirty? And then, you took a taxi to your home, had a shower, and arrived here at around eleven thirty – that is, approximately an hour ago?" The Inspector lifted his arm and checked the time.

"That is about right," I said, realising that the Inspector was eyeing me suspiciously.

"Did you know if Mr Murray was expecting anyone else? Did he mention any such thing to you?"

"Not that I can remember. He did mention, of course, that he would try to get in touch with Miss Hamilton. I think he intended to ring her up."

"Did anyone see you leave Mr Murray's residence?"

"Yes, come to think of it, there was someone. When I opened the front door on leaving Mr Murray's place, one of the occupants – at least I imagined he was an occupant – coming into the hotel bumped into me. He was a short, middle-aged man with an odd-looking moustache. We shook hands, and he apologised for the incident."

"Did Mr Murray see you to the door?"

"Yes, indeed."

"Well, that simplifies matters considerably – both for us and for you." The Inspector smiled amiably and emitted a small sigh. His attitude had relaxed sharply. So that was it; the Inspector had been making sure that everything was above board.

"Really, Inspector," I said, "you aren't suspecting that I had anything to do with it?"

The Inspector smiled. "Well, it is necessary, of course, that we investigate all angles." He shrugged and casually waved his hand in front of him to indicate that one could never be sure.

I still felt that the Inspector was concealing something. "Inspector," I said, "I cannot believe that Mr Murray could have taken his own life. He wasn't the type – it is impossible. It must have been an accident."

The Inspector smiled inscrutably. "I didn't say it was a suicide."

Once again, I couldn't help feeling that the Inspector knew much more than he was willing to reveal. The suggestiveness of his words was disturbing. But, of course, I told myself, I should have guessed from the astute Inspector's searching and detailed interrogation of my statement earlier on that there must have been more to it than met the eye. But the idea of Don being murdered, since that seemed to be the implication, seemed even more remote a possibility than that of suicide.

I consoled myself, however, that the Inspector was merely being noncommittal because, as he had indicated earlier, nothing could be known until the autopsy established the cause of death. The Inspector was merely indicating that the cause of death was unknown, and need not have been suicide, although it may have been so. The suddenness of the events had shocked my mind into a state of confusion, and now the whole thing assumed a bizarre character.

My thoughts were interrupted by the Inspector's voice. "Is there anyone else in the house? Are any of the servants in?" He half addressed Celia and then turned to me, as if he expected me to give him the answer in view of Celia's condition. "We may want to ask them a few questions."

Celia was still sobbing. I was going to reply in the negative because I knew Mrs Feston was away on leave, but Celia nodded and said, "Yes, Inspector. Mrs Feston, my housekeeper, just returned this evening after a few days in Croydon."

"May we have a word with her?" the Inspector said.

"She was very tired and went up to bed. I'd rather she wasn't disturbed," Celia said.

"Well, that's all right, then," said the Inspector. "But I will be grateful if you two could drop in at the station tomorrow morning and bring Mrs Feston with you – say, around ten o'clock. Will that suit you?"

"Yes, of course," I said on behalf of both of us.

"Well, in that case, we won't disturb you any longer."

After the Inspector had tendered his respects to Celia and once again expressed his sympathies, he and the Sergeant prepared to leave. I accompanied them to the door and wished them goodnight. When I went back into the sitting room, Celia was sitting on the divan, her face haggard and drenched, her eyes staring vacantly at the wall.

I looked at my watch. It was late, one thirty a.m., and I was tired. But I felt that I couldn't leave Celia alone in that big house virtually all by herself.

"Celia," I said, "shouldn't you try to get some sleep? I shall stay over tonight so you won't be alone. I can make myself quite comfortable on the divan, and I can help myself to a snack from the pantry. You should eat something, too."

Celia rose from her seat, mopping her face with her handkerchief. Her eyes were red and swollen.

"Thank you so much, Ben, but it won't be necessary, really."

It struck me that I had almost forgotten about Don's death. The news of his death had been so surreal that my mind had not quite come to grips with it. After all, I had seen and spoken to him only a few hours back. This was not easy to accept.

The remembrance of it filled me with melancholy. I was very fond of Don, and it was terribly shocking to think of him as a corpse.

"Ben." Celia's voice broke the silence. "I can't bear it. It's been an awful shock." She started to sob all over again.

"Are you sure you wouldn't want me to stay?" I asked.

She shook her head and looked up with her lips pressed into a hard line. "No, I shall be all right. Don't worry about me. I promise, I shall go to bed right away."

"Ring me if you want anything," I said, reluctant to leave.

I picked up my coat, which I had draped on the back of a chair, and bade Celia goodnight.

Chapter 6

The sun streamed through the thin lace curtains, its rays sharp and painful to the eyes. I must have slept well in the numbed state of mind I had been in the previous evening. It was a beautiful summer's day, and from the bright stillness of the house, I could see the street in the distance come to life.

Presently I heard the shuffling of feet outside my door, followed by a discreet knock. It was Tomlinson bringing in my tea, which I always had in bed.

"Come in," I said.

Tomlinson brought in the tray and put it on the bedside table.

"Good morning, sir," he said. "Lovely day."

"Yes, isn't it?" I said, pouring myself a cup of tea.

Tomlinson lingered by the door.

I said, "I've had some terrible news. I am afraid Mr Murray's dead. He was found gassed in his room in London last night."

Don had been a frequent visitor to my home, and old Tomlinson, like most people, had been very fond of him.

"Oh dear," Tomlinson gasped. "This is a shock, sir. I can't believe it. Whatever made him do such a thing? He seemed a happy gentleman."

"Nobody's sure what happened. It may have been an accident."

"Oh my. It must be a terrible shock for the young lady – Mrs Murray, I mean." Tomlinson shook his head dolefully.

"Yes, it's been an awful shock to all of us," I said. "Ask Dodson to have the car ready. I shall want to leave soon after breakfast."

I looked at my watch. It was a quarter to nine. I hastened out of bed. Poor Celia. I couldn't help feeling sorry for her. Life must, indeed, seem bleak to her. She must have awoken by now. The shock of Don's infidelity must have been unbearable, and the news of his death had left her dazed and speechless.

I decided I would ring her up. For a long while there was no answer, and then Celia picked up the phone.

"I hope I didn't wake you," I said. "Did you get some sleep?"

"Yes, I suppose so," she said weakly.

"The Inspector wanted us at the station at ten," I said. "I'll come over to pick you up in half an hour. Will that be all right?"

"Yes. That should be fine."

"Be seeing you. Mrs Feston will have to come too."

I rushed through my ablutions and breakfast and, having given a few instructions to Tomlinson, dashed out to the porch. Dodson was waiting in the car. When he saw me, he scrambled out and came round to open the door for me.

"Craven Manor," I said, settling myself in the back seat. "And hurry."

When I rang the bell, Celia opened the door.

"Hello," I said, and she affected a smile. Her face looked haggard, and her body, which was normally erect, seemed weighed down as if with some crippling infirmity. She wore a simple low-cut green cotton dress with a square neckline. The décolletage was pleasing without being daring.

"Please be seated, Ben," she said. "Would you like a cup of tea?"

I said I would. Mrs Feston came out of the kitchen looking grave and worried. She sat down as Celia left.

"Such terrible news," she said hoarsely. "I can't believe it."

She sat and clasped her hands in her lap. She was an old woman with silvery hair and a lean, angular face that showed her deep concern.

Celia brought in the tea. I poured myself a cup and took a sip. "You'll have to come with us," I said to Mrs Feston.

"Yes, so Celia tells me. What on earth can they want with me?"

"You know how policemen are. They have to question everybody. It's part of their normal routine."

"We'd better be going," Celia said. "There is so much to be done."

Her face suddenly reddened, and she covered it with her hands and stood up. Her grief was evident. Celia picked up the empty cup of tea, which I had left on the table by my side and went into the kitchen.

I watched Mrs Feston, whose heavily lined face looked taut and forlorn. Tears poured down her cheeks, though she did not give the impression of one who was crying. She bore her grief with the strength and dignity of age, but she could not hide her pain.

She said, "Why did this have to happen to Celia of all people? Poor child. My poor child." She stood up resolutely, as if in an effort to master her feelings, and then sat down again.

It occurred to me how full of unpleasant tasks the day was going to be. There would be, of course, the ordeal of being brought face-to-face with Don's dead body, and then all the arrangements for the visitation at the funeral parlour, the burial, and the hundred and one things which would need tidying up. Besides, his wasn't any ordinary death. One never knew what demands the police would make.

There would, of course, be an inquest and, no doubt, some fuss afterwards.

I could hear Celia clearing up the breakfast things. She soon came out of the kitchen and picked up her bag, which had been lying on the sitting room table.

"I am ready," she said. "Shall we go?"

We rose; Mrs Feston led the way and opened the door. Dodson opened the car door for Celia and Mrs Feston, who both sat in the back, and I got in the front.

We arrived at the police station a little before ten a.m. The constable at the door wished us good morning and asked us to follow him. He ushered us into the Inspector's office without delay.

Inspector Hargreaves rose to greet us and bade us sit down, having dismissed a young constable to whom he had been speaking. The Inspector had a grave expression in his eyes, but he forced a smile to his lips. I introduced Mrs Feston to him.

"How do you do?" he said. "Sorry to have to bother you. Just a routine requirement – a few questions, that's all."

He pressed a button and an electric bell buzzed. A constable entered the room. "I'd like you to be ready to record a statement from Mr Benison in a little while," he said. "And could you send in some tea, please?"

The Inspector cleared his throat. "Mrs Murray, I've just been in touch with London regarding your husband's death. I am afraid they want you to identify the body. You will, of course, be going to London, won't you?"

"Yes, I suppose so," Celia said.

I had planned to spare Celia the ordeal of going to London to arrange for Don's body to be brought to Wimbledon. Celia was hardly in a condition to go traipsing about.

"Does she have to, Inspector?" I asked. "Couldn't the identification be made once the body is brought to Wimbledon?"

The Inspector said apologetically, "I know what a terrible inconvenience it is, but, you see, the enquiry into Mr Murray's death may require – er ... more than the usual formalities. As you know, the London police investigating the case must formally satisfy themselves that all aspects of the enquiry are settled without delay. I am sorry. I am sure you understand."

I did understand. It was an official requirement that the identification be attended to by the London Police before disposal of the body could be permitted.

"When do we have to leave?" I asked.

"Preferably later this morning," the Inspector said. "I shall be going over myself in a little while, and you and Celia might wish to come along with me after you make arrangements to take Mrs Feston home. Unless, of course, you wish to make your own arrangements."

"I think that should be fine, Inspector," I said. "When would you like us to be ready?"

"I hope to leave within the hour," he said, "if that will suit you."

"Yes," I said, speaking for both of us. "That should be fine, I think." Celia nodded approval.

"Shall we make it around eleven thirty, then?" the Inspector said. "That is in roughly an hour's time. That should give us time to record your statement, Mr Benison. In the meantime, I'm sure Mrs Feston wouldn't mind obliging me with just a few answers to the usual questions." The Inspector smiled quietly at the old lady.

Mrs Feston said, also smiling, "Anything you wish, Inspector. I can't see what all this is about, but you've got your job to do, I'm sure."

"Now then," the Inspector said, clearing his throat and assuming just the faintest air of formality. "I understand that you were on vacation until yesterday, when you returned to Mrs Murray's?"

"Yes," Mrs Feston said. "I had gone to Croydon. I have a nephew there, and I'd arranged to spend a week with him and his family. I was due to return only this evening, but my nephew was planning to leave with his wife on a visit to some friends who'd invited them for the day. So I decided that it would suit everybody, myself included, if I left the evening before. I took the train a little after tea and arrived back at Craven Manor last evening."

"Can you remember what time it was when you reached home?"

"It was, I think, about nine thirty p.m. when the train came in at the station. I took a taxi and should have reached Craven Manor by ten or thereabouts."

"Was anyone home at Craven Manor when you arrived?"

"Yes, Mrs Murray was in, as I'd expected." Mrs Feston's voice had the slightest edge in it, as if the Inspector's questioning had offended her.

The Inspector was not to be deterred. He said dryly, "Why did you say 'of course' when I asked you if anyone was at home, Mrs Feston? Am I to presume by your reply that Mrs Murray is always in?"

"What I meant, Inspector," Mrs Feston said, a little aggressively, "is that I knew that Mrs Murray would be in – I mean, I thought she would be in. She and Mr Murray don't go out often. Besides, I had known before I had gone to Croydon that Mr Murray would be away working in London, so I was quite certain that Mrs Murray would be at home. She never, as a rule, goes out anywhere without him unless it is to do the shopping during the day. They were such a devoted couple." This recollection had rather upset her. Her voice broke and her eyes filled with tears. She took out a handkerchief from her bag and dabbed her eyes.

The Inspector shuffled his feet and waited politely. "I am sorry, Mrs Feston," he finally said. "Just a few more questions and then we won't bother you anymore. Did Mrs Murray tell you about the happenings of yesterday afternoon – about the woman, and Mr Benison's going to London to meet Mr Murray? Do you know?"

"Yes, Mrs Murray was most upset. She told me everything."

"What time did you retire for the night?"

"I went to bed a little after eleven. I was terribly tired and could hardly keep my head up. Mrs Murray insisted that I get some rest. I had a sandwich on the train and didn't want any dinner."

The purpose behind the Inspector's questions was, of course, to verify Celia's movements – to see whether she was in the house at the time of Don's death. In other words, she was a suspect. But why? Could it be that the Inspector suspected foul play? I too had been subjected to a thorough interrogation the evening before. Could someone have killed Don after all?

I was quite certain that Don would not have taken his own life, but being a solicitor, I had known of some very odd cases of suicide. I knew that a person could behave quite out of character under certain circumstances and that almost anybody could succumb to despair and disillusionment when faced with insurmountable odds. But it would have taken more than the odds which faced Don to drive him to self-destruction.

Could it be murder? But that possibility seemed quite remote, too. If one were to search for motives, then one could think of a number of people who might want to take Don's life. One could say that Adriana Hamilton had a motive – hatred for the man she had alleged was responsible for her being with child and had deserted her. Then, of course, Celia could be said to have a motive, perhaps the strongest: that of the rebuked and deceived wife getting back at her husband. Then again, others as yet unknown may have had good reason to kill Don. Perhaps members of the underworld to which Adriana Hamilton belonged, or, perhaps, one of her jealous suitors.

It may even have been that his being killed had nothing to do with Miss Hamilton at all. To me it seemed very unlikely that she could have been responsible for Don's death. She seemed so young and afraid. She didn't look the type who could carry out such violence. And, of course, Celia was definitely above suspicion, as she wasn't around at the time of death. Then, there was the possibility of an accident – perhaps a leak in the gas pipe.

Well, there was no point in speculation. "Inspector," I said, "has there been any evidence of foul play?"

The Inspector hesitated. "I'm afraid we won't know for certain until after the autopsy. I have been informed that there are certain aspects of the case which would appear to cast some doubts on the nature of Mr Murray's death. The general impression seems to be that Mr Murray's death may have been due to foul play."

So that was it. That was why the Inspector had been so thorough in his questioning.

The Inspector suddenly got up from his seat. "Well," he said expansively, "I am most grateful to you, Mrs Feston. It was indeed very kind of you to be so patient with me. And now, Mr Benison, if you could give your statement"—he turned to me—"we can be on our way."

He rang the bell, and a constable appeared at the door again. "Please show Mr Benison to Inspector Lowland's room," he said.

After I had my statement taken down and had signed it, I went back to Inspector Hargreaves's office. A constable produced my statement, and the Inspector read it. "Yes, that about covers everything," he said, handing the statement back to the constable.

Celia and Mrs Feston had remained with the Inspector while I had been away, and they were still seated as I had left them. I knew that the Inspector must have questioned Celia too. She sat hunched in her chair and seemed quite spent and oblivious to everything going on around her. It was indeed an ordeal to be bothered with questions at a time of tragedy.

"We shall leave in half an hour," the Inspector said, standing. "Would that be all right, Mrs Murray?"

Celia nodded and smiled faintly at him. "Yes, thank you, Inspector. That should be fine."

I took Celia's arm and left the room, Mrs Feston following.

"Ben," Celia said, "could we drop in at the garage and ask a mechanic to have a look at my car? I think we may need to have it ready for tomorrow."

"Yes," I said, thinking of the funeral arrangements. "I think we'd better attend to it."

Celia paused until Mrs Feston caught up with us. "Darling, we won't be long. There's a little matter to be attended to. Could you wait here until we've done?"

"Yes," Mrs Feston said. "I'll be quite comfortable here. Take your time."

"There is a little garage close by," Celia said to me. "They attend to all my repairs."

We stepped into the car, and I directed Dodson to the address Celia gave me.

It was a moderately sized garage in which three men were busily working on a lorry parked near the entrance. Another man stood peering into the engine of a car parked next to the lorry. They were all wearing grey overalls splotched with black patches of oil and grease.

We went in through an arched entrance. A number of cars were parked under a zinc-sheeted roof supported by iron girders.

To our right as we entered was a small office with the words "No Admittance" on the door. Adjoining it was another room with yellow square mesh running along a low wall. The room held an aluminium table and three foam-rubber-cushioned settees. At the entrance to the garage proper was a sign with the words "Please do not block the way of other cars" painted in white on a blackboard. The words "Engine Overhauling" were written on one of the walls. Cars were parked in neat rows, and some of them were being worked on. There was quite a lot of activity and no small din: the clang of hammer against metal, the revving of engines being tested, and the screeching of lathes.

From somewhere among the cars a man wearing a red sweater and khaki trousers came towards us. He seemed friendly. He smiled as he saw Celia and said, "Good morning." He must have known her.

"What is it we can do for you, Mrs Murray?" he said cheerfully, his gaunt, middle-aged face wrinkling as his toothy smile widened. The din was quite infuriating, and even though he yelled, it was an effort to hear him. "Shall we go into the lounge?" the man said, covering his ears with hands to indicate that we had better get away from the noise.

Celia explained that the car was once again out of order and that it wouldn't start.

"Aha," the man said, "same trouble as last time, it seems to me." He scratched his head. "Did you try tightening the battery terminals?"

"No," Celia answered. "Could you send someone to check it, please? I need the car by tomorrow. I must have it ready by then. I am on my way to London."

"Oh!" the man said, his face showing his dismay. "You could have tried it. Those terminals could be the cause. All right, I'll send someone up this afternoon. Will Mr Murray be in?"

"No," Celia said, biting her lip. "No, but my housekeeper, Mrs Feston, will be in. I'll leave the car keys with her."

Chapter 7

Back at the station, the Inspector kept glancing at his watch, obviously impatient to get to London, and soon we were on our way. I had accepted the Inspector's offer to ride with him because I disliked taking my car into London. It was much more convenient to use a taxi or public transport there.

It was almost lunchtime when we reached the city centre. "Go straight to the mortuary at St Mary's Hospital in Paddington," the Inspector said to the driver sotto voce. "We are expected there."

The car turned left and entered the Paddington area.

Soon after, the car stopped in front of an ancient grey building, and we got out. We reached the mortuary through a side entrance. The Inspector rang the bell, and the door opened to reveal an attendant in blue overalls, galoshes, and a white apron. The Inspector and the attendant exchanged a few words, and the Inspector nodded. He then walked across a courtyard, with us following at his heels, and through a doorway marked "Private. Doctors only," which led into the mortuary.

I held Celia's arm firmly and reassuringly. My own heart was beating loudly. It wouldn't be long now before Don's body would be exposed to our eyes.

The Inspector slowed down and waited for Celia. He gently took her other arm.

"The body is in there," he said, pointing to the door of the mortuary. "You must be brave. It won't take a moment."

The attendant pushed open the door and stood aside to let us in. We were at once assailed by the odour of disinfectant and the sickening smell of decay and corruption. It made my stomach turn. Two bodies lay on gleaming white marble tables, each with their heads propped on small blocks of wood.

At the table nearest the door, a man stood wearing a white gown, a rubber apron, and rubber gloves. I guessed he was the pathologist. He was talking to a man in a grey suit and mackintosh. The latter came up to us when he saw us. He greeted Inspector Hargreaves silently and led us to the table on which Don's body lay. The body was covered with a shroud, with only the face exposed. Both Celia and I identified it as Don's.

It was strange and awesome to see Don's dead body. It seemed so incredible that he should be dead when only yesterday he had seemed so alive. In death his face looked severe, the heightened pallor of his skin giving it a sculptured appearance.

Celia put a handkerchief to her wet eyes and, lowering her head, stared in disbelief at the dead face of the man who despite all his faults had once been her husband. After a while she turned away and walked out of the room. We followed her out in silence, carrying with us the sense of doom that pervades the minds of the living at the sight of the dead.

We drove off in Inspector Hargreaves's car to the Paddington police station.

Once there, Inspector Hargreaves knocked on an opaque glass door which bore the name "Inspector Blythe, AB" with "CID" printed above it.

When we entered, Inspector Hargreaves introduced us to Inspector Blythe, a thin bespectacled man. He in turn introduced us to a short burly man who was standing by the window when we came in. He had bushy eyebrows; a long, quivering nose; and thin lips hidden under the arbour of a heavy mustache that sprouted out in all directions. Inspector Blythe introduced him to us as Detective Chief Inspector Smith from Scotland Yard.

His being from the Yard struck me as rather portentous, and my fears were borne out when Inspector Blythe informed us that the Chief Inspector had come down specially to enquire into Don's death. Seeing that his statement called for some explanation, Blythe motioned for us to sit down and commenced to acquaint us with the situation.

"We all know that this has been an awful shock for you, Mrs Murray, but you must be prepared for a further shock." He paused. "We have been informed that the autopsy shows beyond doubt that the death of your husband was due to carbon monoxide poisoning, but the police investigation and other circumstances seem to indicate that Mr Murray could not have taken his own life and that death could not have been due to an accident. Our suspicion is, therefore, that there has been some foul play."

I looked across at Celia. She was seated with her hands in her lap, her fingers clutching her handkerchief fiercely. Her face was intense and white. On hearing Blythe's pronouncement, she looked up for a brief moment, as if she had been suddenly jolted into awareness by what she had heard. Then she resumed that faraway, enervated look.

Inspector Blythe cleared his throat. I couldn't restrain my curiosity.

"Inspector," I said, "what evidence is there to indicate foul play?"

Blythe folded his hands in front of him, and his eyes became alert. "I was coming to that, Mr Benison," he said. "However, I think the Chief Inspector can give you a better answer than I can. Would you, Chief Inspector?"

He turned deferentially to the Chief Inspector, who nodded and said, "Yes, yes of course." He folded his sturdy arms over his chest and addressed us quietly, in a clear, metallic voice.

"You see, the circumstances of Mr Murray's death are indeed strange – very strange. When the police arrived at the scene, there was a strong smell of gas. However, on examining the gas tap in Mr Murray's room, they found that it was quite secure. Someone had obviously closed it. They questioned the maid, who had been the first person to sound the alarm. She said that she was walking along the corridor outside Mr Murray's room when she detected the strong odour. Her suspicion was aroused, and she knocked on Mr Murray's door but found it was locked."

The Chief Inspector went on to explain that the maid had been caught in a grip of panic and had immediately run down to Mrs Bleakely, the landlady, who lived in a basement room, and she had opened the door to Mr Murray's room with the house key.

When she opened the door, she too was assailed by the strong smell of gas, and when she saw the body of Mr Murray lying motionless on the bed, she naturally assumed the worst.

Mrs Bleakely immediately rang up the police. She was quite certain that neither she nor the maid had made any attempt to open the windows or close the gas tap. Both she and the maid affirmed that in the confusion of the moment, it had completely slipped their minds to do so.

The Chief Inspector wiped his face slowly and deliberately with a clean white handkerchief and carefully replaced it in his pocket. "When the police arrived on the scene, they exercised a great deal of caution in handling the gas tap so as not to obliterate any prints – the usual procedure, you know – and, of course, they found the gas tap closed and no gas leakage. Subsequent examination for prints on the tap revealed an interesting fact – namely, that there weren't any fingerprints on it at all. This, of course, more or less confirmed the testimony of the maid and Mrs Bleakely that they had not meddled with the tap. The lack of prints indicated to investigators that whoever had opened and shut the tap must have been wearing gloves or else had taken the precaution to wipe it clean.

"On arriving at the scene, the police made a further curious observation. They found a glass on the deceased's dressing table which smelt of whisky. The autopsy report confirmed that the deceased had consumed whisky but revealed also that he had taken a strong sleeping draught. An examination of the remnants in the glass confirmed that there were traces of the sleeping draught. But it has been established that the dose the deceased took was not lethal. In fact, although it was a strong dose, it happened to be completely harmless, as the cause of the death was carbon monoxide poisoning.

"Now, let us say that the deceased wished to kill himself. Let us also assume that he first took a sleeping draught, for reasons best known to himself, and gassed himself. Now, if his intention was suicide, would he have knocked off the gas tap after having opened it? But, let's assume for argument's sake that he suddenly changed his mind – perhaps when it was a bit too late? If that were so, it is highly unlikely, isn't it, that we should find the deceased snug in his bed with the sheets pulled neatly over him? If the deceased had changed his mind at the last minute, there should have been evidence of a certain disorder and the marks of confusion as would have resulted from the deceased having hurriedly closed the tap, and, considering the amount of gas in his body, having doddered, at best, to his bed. Also, why would he have taken the trouble to wipe his fingerprints from the tap? It seems unlikely to us, therefore, that the deceased took his own life.

"However, even though we suspect foul play, there is one issue that has had us completely baffled – the same issue, in fact, which has led us to believe that Mr Murray could not have taken his own life."

There was a pause, filled with suspense, before the Chief Inspector continued. "The issue concerns the closed gas tap. Paradoxically, if the fact of the tap being closed absolves the deceased from having taken his own life, it also makes us hard put to explain why anyone who may have opened the tap bothered to close it. Yet the fact that it was closed has, ironically, supplied us with the only hint that the deceased could not have done it himself, or to put it more explicitly, that someone other than the deceased must have done so."

"I see what you mean, Chief Inspector," I said. "But if, as you suggest, some unknown person opened the gas tap, then such a supposition poses certain problems. How could anyone have remained in the room, as he must have done if he had also, as we must presume, shut the tap himself, with such a volume of gas afloat without having endangered himself? And then, of course, as you yourself pointed out, why should such a person have shut the tap? If the tap had not been shut, it is quite likely that the whole thing would have given the appearance of suicide. As it is, the murderer has by his conduct brought attention to himself in the most obvious manner possible."

"Precisely," replied the Chief Inspector. "That is what's so baffling. That is what we must find out." He coughed into his handkerchief. He pulled out a leather cigarette case from his pocket and offered one to Celia and then me. I declined. When he spoke again, his manner and tone had assumed a more formal air

"Mr Benison," he said, "we have just seen the statement you made to the Wimbledon Police, and we need to ask you a few more questions. We should also want to clarify one or two matters with you, Mrs Murray – just a formality, you know." The Chief Inspector smiled genially, flashing his white teeth under his bushy moustache. "In the meantime, of course, while Mr Benison is with us, I am sure you'd rather have some time to yourself."

He rang the bell, and a constable opened the door. "Please show Mrs Murray to the restroom. I am sure she'd like a cup of tea."

Chapter 8

Once we were alone, Chief Inspector Smith faced me with a purposeful glint in his eyes.

"Right-oh," he said, pursing his lips, "just a few questions. As I said, I have read your statement to the Wimbledon Police." He tapped the file that lay on his desk. "And there are one or two matters that need clarification.

"You say that you arrived at Mr Murray's place at about seven fifteen p.m. on the sixteenth of July and that you stayed with him for about forty-five minutes. Then, you visited a pub and went to dinner with a Mr James Falkland from around eight thirty p.m. to a little past nine and thereafter took the train to Wimbledon at approximately nine forty-five. Is that correct?"

I confirmed that the details were correct. The Chief Inspector then asked me for Mr Falkland's address, which I gave him.

"And you reached Wimbledon at approximately ten thirty p.m.?"

"Yes, but as I have said in my statement, it must have been around eleven thirty at least before I reached Mrs Murray's because I went home first and had a shower and a change of clothes."

"Did Mr Murray say that he was going to contact Miss Hamilton on that very evening?"

"Yes. He seemed anxious to get in touch with her to straighten things out."

"Did he express any intention of ringing her up?"

"Yes, he said he would give her a call that very night."

"I am afraid we've had some difficulty in locating her address. No one seems to know anything about her. Have you any idea where she lives?"

I explained that I did not know her address but that Don had indicated that she was staying in a flat behind the Bayswater Tube station. I told him Don's story, including that she was a prostitute.

The Chief Inspector was pleased with this information. He assured me that if she was still living in the same area, there shouldn't be any difficulty in ferreting her out. The local police may have already had occasion to know of her if she was a woman of the streets.

"Also," I said, "she might get in touch with me tomorrow for the £5,000, which she has been hankering after, mightn't she?"

"Not on your nelly," the Chief Inspector said, grinning broadly. "I have a hunch that she would have heard by now about Mr Murray's death and wouldn't want to be mixed up in anything to do with him. News travels much faster than one imagines, I assure you. Besides, the newspapers have already got their hands on this business, and it should be common knowledge by this evening. The *Times* has already sent a man to report on Mr Murray's death."

"I hadn't thought of that," I said.

"One more question," the Chief Inspector said. "Do you think Mr Murray could have taken his own life?"

"No," I said. "I don't think the thought would have even occurred to him."

"Well, thank you, Mr Benison. You've been very helpful. We are indeed sorry for all the inconvenience."

"Not at all," I said. "I am only too glad to be of service. Mr Murray was a very good and long-standing friend of mine, and naturally I am most anxious that whoever may have been responsible for his death be brought to book."

Inspector Blythe, who had been silently observing from one of the chairs, whispered something into the Chief Inspector's ear. The latter nodded and turned to me. "You must forgive me, Mr Benison, but you may have to spare us a little more of your time. You see, we will have to check out your story that you were seen leaving Mr Murray's hotel by one of the occupants. Just a routine requirement, but it's important. It's in your own interest that we corroborate this. After all, you were the last person, as far as we know, to see Mr Murray alive. If you could come along with us to the Clarendon, we could try to locate the tenant in question and see if you can identify him. Being a Sunday, it is possible that he may be in."

"Certainly, Chief Inspector," I said. "I shall be most happy to be of assistance."

"Incidentally," he said, "we have in the meantime just corroborated with Mr Falkland your account of your meeting with him."

I understood only too well that the police's enquiries had to begin with me. After all, as the Chief Inspector had pointed out, I was the last person known to have met with Don, and the maid had discovered his dead body less than two and a half hours after I had left his room.

"Isn't there going to be an inquest?" I asked.

"Yes, of course," the Chief Inspector said. "I meant to tell you about it. It's scheduled for Monday at nine thirty. Mrs Murray and you will need to be there, but there can't be any doubt that it will be adjourned for the police to make enquiries. That is when the press will take over. With the adjournment of the inquest, the newspapers will really splash the news about."

"That will be terrible," I said. Such a lot of publicity would bring Celia and me into the public eye. Nothing would be spared – not the sordid facts of Don's private life – and the speculation and insinuations, even accusations, would erupt around us and isolate us. It would be especially cruel for Celia. Reporters wouldn't give her any peace, and the airing of her dirty linen would destroy her privacy for a long time to come.

The Chief Inspector said, "I should not give any interviews, if I were you. And I think it would be best if Mrs Murray hid from the press as soon as the inquest is over. Has she anywhere to stay in London?"

"Yes, she could stay at her aunt's at Shepherd's Bush. She will be most welcome there. Her aunt and uncle live alone and pretty much keep to themselves. I think she will be safe there."

The Chief Inspector rang the desk bell. A constable arrived at the door. "Call Mrs Murray in," he said.

"You could stay if you wish," he said, addressing me. "It might be of help to Mrs Murray if you did."

Celia came in ushered by the constable who had been sent to bring her. The Chief Inspector half rose from his seat and asked her to be seated in front of his desk.

"Mrs Murray, we won't keep you long. Just a few brief questions which will help us." The Chief Inspector leaned over the desk, and his voice was gentle and low. "How often was it necessary … how often did your husband stay in London?"

"At least twice a month. Sometimes more. He was on the board of trustees for schools run by the Church of England and was also actively involved in the administrative aspects and overall management of the schools. He also acted as inspector of schools. He said it was necessary that he stay over for a day or two at a time, sometimes for as much as three or four days."

"He could have travelled daily from Wimbledon, though, couldn't he?"

Celia lowered her head. "Yes, I suppose he could have. At the start he nearly always did, but in the last five or six months, he stayed over more often. He said it was more convenient, as he finished late and had too many files to cart around."

The Chief Inspector cleared his throat. "Did you suspect that anything was wrong?"

"No," Celia said, shaking her head. "He always gave me very plausible explanations, and I believed him. I did go and stay with him once or twice at the start, but I did not wish to disturb his work."

"Did he always know when you were coming over, or did you sometimes visit him without prior arrangement?"

"My visits were, of course, usually by prior arrangement. But I have on occasion dropped in on him without his expecting me. You know, just to give him a surprise. There were also odd occasions when I decided to do some shopping in London and was not able to reach him in his office or hotel to inform him in advance of my arrival."

"How many such surprise visits did you pay him? Can you remember the number?"

Celia paused awhile. She looked up at the ceiling as she tried to recall. "Well … er … thrice, to be exact."

"Did you find him in on these occasions?"

"Yes, except once. But I didn't have to wait long then. He'd been out for a walk in the park, and I must have waited for an hour at the most."

"Wasn't it a bit risky your visiting him as you did without first letting him know? I mean, he may have gone out, and I would expect that would mean you were kept waiting literally on your feet until he arrived."

"Not really; I wouldn't have had to stand around. Don always kept his key on the outside ledge of the door to his room. It was a sort of habit for him. He used to say that he hated carrying keys on him because they were inconvenient and cumbersome."

"Wasn't he concerned that someone might open his room in his absence – a thief, for instance?"

"No, I don't think Don let such a consideration worry him. After all, he was only in residence for a few days at a time, and there wasn't really anything in the room worth taking."

"Yes, I suppose you're right." The Chief Inspector rose from his seat and thanked Celia. "We shan't keep you any longer," he said.

I exchanged a few words with the Chief Inspector. He said that we would go over to the Clarendon later in the afternoon. I said I would join him after I had deposited Celia at her aunt's and had a bite for lunch. Inspector Hargreaves, who returned to the room after having got some coffee, shook hands with us and informed us that he had to return to Wimbledon. He said he would be glad to be of any assistance if we needed him once we returned.

Now that we were in London, the matter was outside his jurisdiction.

We took a taxi to Shepherd's Bush. Celia's paternal aunt, Mrs Haversham, was a gentle lady who doted on Celia. She and her husband, who was a retired teacher, were very old, had no children of their own, and lived in a delightful three-bedroom house.

Celia knocked on the door and her aunt opened it, a smile crossing her face at the sight of Celia. But the sad expression on Celia's face and her puffy eyes immediately told Mrs Haversham that something was wrong.

It was I who broke the news to her. She showed Celia to her room and came back to meet me in the hall.

"Such shocking news," she said, shaking her silvery head. "So selfish of him, suicide. What is to become of her? Oh, my poor child."

Mrs Haversham belonged to a generation who were hardy of spirit and mind and whose lives were steady though staid. To them, suicide was disgraceful, an unpardonable crime. They employed no subtleties in condemning it – it was cowardly and selfish.

I had only mentioned that Don had been found dead in his room from gas poisoning. Mrs Haversham had assumed it was suicide. I didn't think it was necessary for me to mention that it may have been murder.

Mr Haversham was not in. He would, she said, be back from the grocer's any time now. "What arrangements are you making for the funeral?" she said.

Actually, with the shock of the news and the visit to the police, there hadn't been any time at all in which to discuss the arrangements. I had, however, been thinking it over and had decided that it would be best, if Celia were willing, for the obsequies to be done here in London. Such an arrangement would be the most convenient.

For one thing, there was the inquest, at which our presence was required. All in all, it would be less unpleasant and more expeditious to have it done in London. There would, of course, have to be the necessary announcement in the papers and notifications to a few of Don's friends and relatives by telephone or telegram.

I explained my idea to Mrs Haversham, and she agreed with it. She said that she would undertake to speak to Celia on the matter, and I promised to make whatever arrangements were necessary for Don's cremation. The ashes could later be laid to rest in Wimbledon. I bade Mrs Haversham goodbye and took a taxi to meet Chief Inspector Smith.

Chapter 9

The Clarendon's landlady, Mrs Bleakely, opened the door for us. She was a short, stout, red-faced woman with an unwashed face and uncombed hair. She smiled obliquely at the sight of the Chief Inspector and his retinue, which included Inspector Blythe and a Detective Sergeant Holmes from the Yard, and nervously smoothed her hands over her dress and over her hair to tidy herself.

"Good afternoon," said Inspector Blythe. "We've come to have another look at Mr Murray's room. We are sorry to inconvenience you." He did not bother to introduce the Chief Inspector or Sergeant Holmes.

"Not your fault, is it?" Mrs Bleakely said in a gruff voice. She led the way down the corridor. A constable stood guard at the entrance to Don's room. He saluted us smartly and stood aside for the detectives to make their entry.

"Thank you," Inspector Blythe said, turning to Mrs Bleakely. "That will be all for now. We would like a few words with you in a little while, though, if you don't mind."

"Not at all, Inspector," said Mrs Bleakely wearily. "I'll be downstairs in my room if you want me."

Chief Inspector Smith stood in front of the door and, looking up, ran his hand along the top of the doorframe. His hand halted. When he brought it down, there was a key in it.

"Well," the Chief Inspector said, clapping the dust from his hands and holding up the silver key between his thumb and index finger. "This bears out Mrs Murray's statement."

He popped the key into the air, caught it, and whipped it into his coat pocket.

I followed the Chief Inspector, Inspector Blythe, and Detective Sergeant Holmes into Don's room. It looked exactly as I had remembered it, except for a slight disarray, which, no doubt, had been caused by the police inspection and search. The area around the bed had been cordoned off with yellow tape.

Inspector Blythe led me to a dressing table beside the wardrobe. It was on this, the Inspector informed me, that the glass with the whisky and sleeping draught had been found. The glass had been taken away for examination. To the left of the dressing table was the gas heater.

Don's bed lay close to the heater – the headboard was not five feet from it. It would have been a matter of minutes before the gas had killed him.

Inspector Blythe said, looking around him, "Whoever planned it was very clever indeed. We are up against someone very cunning. What a perfect set-up for suicide. The psychological climate was just right – Mr Murray was the victim of blackmail, putting his marriage and his job in jeopardy; the only prints on the glass were his; and only one glass had been drunk from, the one from which Mr Murray had taken the draught. The presence of only one glass indicates, of course, that there was nobody else in the room and points the finger strongly in Mr Murray's direction. But as I always say, some indiscretion always gives the show away."

The Inspector fetched out his pigskin cigarette case from his coat pocket, selected a cigarette, and put it to his lips. He patted his trouser pockets, dug his hand into one of them, pulled out a faded lighter, and lit his cigarette with a steady hand.

"Most curious it was, I can assure you," the Inspector said after blowing out a long stream of smoke. "There he was, so cosily tucked up in bed, with the sheets hardly disturbed, as if he'd crept in with the greatest of care. It was too good to be true. How would a man who had drugged himself and inhaled enough gas as to kill him have been in a condition to step into his bed after having closed the gas tap? But the fact that there were no signs of disarray does seem to suggest this, doesn't it?"

Detective Sergeant Holmes said, as if to himself, "I think it's only a question of time before we get our man, or woman, as the case may be. I think we have a reasonable general description of the criminal in our minds already. He or she must have been someone who knew the deceased well, someone who had in all probability visited this room before and knew its layout – where the gas tap was, for instance – and someone, in fact, who had been—" Holmes broke off suddenly and scratched the back of his balding head as if some tricky question had just cropped up in his mind. His plump, florid face assumed a perplexed expression.

"What is it, Holmes?" the Chief Inspector said. "Got a brain wave, have you?"

"I was just thinking, sir," Holmes said, still scratching his head, "whoever did it must have had to be sure that Mr Murray would consent to having a drink – otherwise, he wouldn't have been able to knock him off, would he?"

"Yes, Holmes," the Chief Inspector said. "You have a point there. If the murderer had come prepared to administer a sleeping draught and intended to make the death look like suicide, as we think was the case, then he would have rather been up a gum tree if Mr Murray had not wanted a drink. What looks a bit odd, though, is that he had managed to get Mr Murray to take a drink without himself having taken one. But, there could be a simple explanation for that. Our murderer may have known that Mr Murray would offer him a drink – it was probably his practice to take a drink in the evenings – so all our criminal had to do was refuse it once he was quite sure that Mr Murray was going to have one anyway. You may be right, Holmes. Whoever it was probably was pretty familiar with the deceased's habits."

"I think you are right there, Chief Inspector," I interpolated. "Mr Murray was in the habit of taking a drink as the evening waned. In fact, he did offer me a drink, which I refused, when I saw him last evening, as I've mentioned in my statement. He always kept a bottle with him. He didn't take a drink when he offered me one, though. Said he preferred to drink a little later in the evening."

The Chief Inspector took charge. He turned towards the door and addressed the young constable standing just outside it. "Simpson," he said, "go down and call Mrs Bleakely, will you?"

When Mrs Bleakely came, the Chief Inspector led her into the small lounge in the centre of the house, which looked as if it had never been used. Everything seemed to be exactly in place, and there was a faint odour of mustiness in the air as if it had not been dusted and aired in years.

It was a small room with a rusty fire grate and mildewed furniture. The red covers hung loosely on the settees. When everybody had seated themselves, the Chief Inspector asked Mrs Bleakely to describe everything she recalled concerning the incident. She had already made a statement that explained that the maid had informed her concerning Don and that she had called the police. She said it was one of those rare days when she had gone out in the evening. As a rule, she said, she hardly went out, as she was afflicted with arthritis in her legs, causing her great pain when she walked. She was nearly always confined to her room and did not, therefore, know very much about the goings and comings of the tenants or their friends. She lived in a back room in the basement, which further isolated her from the rest of the household and put her well out of earshot of any of the boarders. She explained that there were no boarders in the basement, which, besides her room, contained only a storeroom, a kitchen, and a lounge where boarders took breakfast.

Once she got started, Mrs Bleakely was not easy to stop. We listened on without interrupting her.

She said that Mr Murray had stayed in her rooming house whenever he stayed over in London. She had always a room or two vacant, as people were always coming and going on short visits, and Mr Murray always booked his room in advance. She thought he was such a nice gentleman – always so courteous and cheerful – that she had generally tried to reserve for him, whenever possible, the large ground-floor room in which he had been staying, as it was one of the best rooms in the hotel. He always tipped her handsomely and once brought her flowers and a box of chocolates to cheer her up.

He had told her that Mrs Murray liked coming down to London sometimes at the weekend when he was in London, and Mrs Bleakely had once actually emerged from her room and knocked on Mr Murray's door on the pretext of requiring something just to see how his wife looked. She had found Mrs Murray in the room with Mr Murray, and Mr Murray had introduced them and they had spoken a few words. She thought that Mrs Murray must, indeed, be lucky to be the wife of such a kind and handsome man. She hadn't seen Mrs Murray after that, but she had heard from Mr Murray that she had come to see him once or twice thereafter.

142 Wellington Place

The Chief Inspector cleared his throat and said, "Tell me, Mrs Bleakely, do you know if anybody besides Mrs Murray ever called on Mr Murray?"

"Not that I know of, but then, as I said, I don't come up very often. Although ... yes, someone did call on him once. A few weeks back, I was leaving the house for some shopping when there was a lady outside his door who asked me if Mr Murray was in. She had rung his bell and hadn't got any reply. She wanted to know if he had left his lodgings and when he was expected back. She seemed to know that he took lodgings here when he was in London. She was some foreign girl – and very attractive and well dressed, I must say."

"Did any of the other tenants visit his room?"

"Oh, yes, there was Mrs Blaine, who was in the room next door to him. She left only yesterday. Poor thing. She had some bad news concerning her nephew. He was in some accident and had to be rushed to hospital. Imagine her leaving the very night of Mr Murray's death. She would have been most upset if she had been here when we found him dead. In fact, that was just a little past ten p.m., and she was lucky to have been spared that ordeal."

This seemed to arouse the Chief Inspector's curiosity. His manner, which was phlegmatic as always, did not betray this, but a slight inflection in his voice hinted that he was more than normally interested. "When did Mrs Blaine leave?" he asked.

"Well, I'm not certain. It must have been around ten last night. I had stepped out for about half an hour at nine thirty to buy some pills from the chemist and have some fish and chips. When I came back at about ten fifteen, I found an envelope under my door. There was a note in it from Mrs Blaine explaining that she was sorry to have missed me but that she had to leave without any delay and explaining her nephew's accident."

"Did she say where she was going?"

"No, there was no mention of that."

"Have you got the note with you?"

"No, I am afraid I tore it up and threw it away."

"Did she indicate whether she would be back?"

"No. She had paid for her room at the beginning of the week, and she said she would probably be away for some time but would write and let me know when she was ready to come back."

The young constable standing guard outside Don's door cleared his throat to announce his presence and tiptoed into the lounge. He spoke a few words to Detective Sergeant Holmes, who nodded and approached the Chief Inspector.

"Simpson's here, sir. Just had a word with him. He says a Miss Proust, one of the occupants, would like a word with you. Says she's got some information that may be of some use to the police."

The Chief Inspector looked up. "She has, has she? Well, send her in." He turned to Mrs Bleakely. "Thank you very much, Mrs Bleakely. That will be all for now."

"Thank you, Chief Inspector," Mrs Bleakely said. She stood with some effort and ambled out of the room.

Simpson had re-entered the lounge followed by a tall, lanky woman in an ill-fitting blue dress which accentuated her extreme thinness and the flatness of her chest. She had a long face with high cheekbones. Her mousy hair had been pulled back into a bun, giving her face a decidedly horsey appearance. She carried her head very straight, and her general manner seemed very prim and proper.

"Please be seated," the Chief Inspector said. "Is there something you wish to tell us?"

"Yes, Chief Inspector, I thought there was something you should know, though it may not be of any value, really."

The Chief Inspector waited for Miss Proust to continue.

"What I have to say concerns the evening of Mr Murray's death. Around nine p.m., after a cup of coffee, I left my room and decided I would come down and borrow a few magazines from Mrs Blaine. You see, I live on the third floor. Actually, I didn't know Mrs Blaine very well. We had met on a few occasions in the lounge here after dinner – as a rule, no one ever comes up here, but I used to read here now and again, as I found it quiet and homey. You know, not as confining as one's room. Mrs Blaine would drop in on rare occasions with a pile of magazines – mostly women's weeklies and the like. We got to talking and we used to lend each other reading material from time to time. I had gone down to her room once or twice for brief spells just to borrow a magazine or two for the night and to lend her a book of my own. Anyway, on this particular evening I knocked on Mrs Blaine's door but there was no reply. I was about to leave when I thought I heard a woman cough in the adjoining room – Mr Murray's room, that is. It sounded very much like Mrs Blaine. You see, she suffered from bronchitis and was given on occasion to fits of coughing."

Miss. Proust paused awhile to wipe her nose with a handkerchief she extracted from her dress pocket. "Naturally, I presumed that Mrs Blaine had dropped in to see Mr Murray. She had told me that she dropped in on him on occasion. He seemed to be friendly to her. I decided I'd go back to my room. Halfway up the second flight of stairs, I thought I heard the door to Mr Murray's room open and shut. I stopped and listened in case Mrs Blaine could be going back to her room, but instead I distinctly heard the sound of footsteps going away, and then I heard the front door open and shut. I thereafter returned to my room and went to bed."

The Chief Inspector said, "Have you any reason to suspect that Mrs Blaine had anything to do with Mr Murray's death?"

"Oh, no," Miss Proust rejoined. "Nothing of the sort. I merely thought there might be some connection. After all …"

"Of course, Miss Proust, naturally you were quite right. If Mrs Blaine had been in Mr Murray's room on the evening of his death, then that certainly would arouse one's suspicion. Especially so now that Mrs Blaine has disappeared and seems to have left in a hurry."

"Yes, yes, Chief Inspector, that is how I felt."

The Chief Inspector leaned forward with an intense look on his face and said, "Can you be sure it was Mrs Blaine?"

"Well, naturally, I cannot say I am certain since I didn't see her, but I thought I recognised Mrs Blaine's cough and, besides, I am sure she couldn't have been in her room."

"What time was it?"

"It was a little past nine."

"Didn't it strike you as rather odd that Mrs Blaine should have been in Mr Murray's room at such an hour?"

"Not really. I've seen them together in the corridor. They seemed to know each other well. At any rate, Mr Murray seemed very friendly. And as I said, she told me that she did drop in on Mr Murray on occasion."

The Chief Inspector sat up straight. "What do you know about Mrs Blaine, Miss Proust? Had you known her for long? Did she tell you about herself – you know, how she supported herself, where she was from, that sort of thing?"

"I am afraid my relationship with Mrs Blaine was a very casual one. She was just an acquaintance, and we hardly had occasion to discuss personal matters. To the best of my knowledge, she didn't leave the building much. On the few occasions I've stayed away from work on leave, I noticed her leave the house quite late in the day. I came to know her only about three weeks back – that is, a few days after she came to stay here. I myself have been here for over three months now."

"How old was she?"

"I'd say about fifty, but it was difficult to say. She may have been younger. You see, she looked emaciated and quite worn out."

"You say you had occasion to visit her room, Miss Proust? Did you notice any photographs?"

"She did have two photographs on her dressing table. One was of a boy of about ten years of age. The other was one of herself standing with her arm around the boy. I am afraid I didn't enquire who he was."

"Is there anything else that you think may be of value? Was there anything about her that you feel we should know?"

"No, I don't think there's anything else, really. Well ... I don't know. Er ... perhaps it isn't fair to say, really. It is only an opinion, and it can hardly be of value ..."

"Everything is of value at this stage, Miss Proust," the Chief Inspector said persuasively.

"Well, in that case, Chief Inspector, I'd better say what I think. She seemed a nice enough person to me, but there was something about her that was well ... er ... degenerate. Yes, I am afraid that is the only word I can think of which will describe her. Mind you, I am not saying that she did anything to give me such an impression. She merely looked it. I don't mean just her physical appearance, but her manner and the way she dressed. Her clothes were always a trifle garish, and her face always made up with too much lipstick and rouge. It was really as artificial as a mask. Her manners were somewhat coarse and bawdy, and her speech loud and vulgar. She made one feel a little repulsed, if you know what I mean."

"Thank you, Miss Proust. You've been most helpful. That will be all for now."

When Miss Proust had left the room, the Chief Inspector asked that the maid, Miss Caverill, be brought in.

Simpson brought her in. She was in her early thirties, very thin, and a little hunched. Her face was pinched and quite anaemic.

She sat down at the Chief Inspector's bidding and placed her hands in her lap, her fingers twining about each other nervously.

"Now, Miss Caverill," the Chief Inspector said, "we already have your statement. I want to ask just a few general questions." He cleared his throat. "How long have you worked here as a maid?"

"More than four years. Five years this December."

"Did you have occasion to speak to the deceased, Mr Murray?"

"No. I usually clean up the rooms after the tenants leave for work in the mornings."

"Would you be able to say if Mr Murray had any visitors? Anyone who came looking for him or who rang him up?"

"Not that I know of. I hardly get to see anything of the tenants, really. You see, I work only during the day and am off in the evenings, except on the Saturdays when I work the night shift. That is how I was able to discover the smell of gas from Mr Murray's room yesterday."

"How did you come to discover that there was a gas leak?"

"Well, I had finished my supper and decided around ten to visit the coffee shop at the corner for a cup of coffee. I often do that, as an outing last thing at night, before turning in. Well, as I passed by Mr Murray's room, there was a strong smell of gas, so I knocked at his door to see if anything was wrong but got no reply. So I decided I should tell Mrs Bleakely, who had just returned from outside, and we both came up, and she opened the door, and that's when we realised poor Mr Murray was dead. It was awful, I can tell you. So Mrs Bleakely called the police immediately and they were here in less than ten minutes."

"Well, thank you, Miss Caverill. But what of Mrs Blaine? Can you tell us say anything about her?"

"Well, now she was an odd woman. She'd been in the hotel only a month or so at the most. I had my doubts about her, I must say."

"Just what do you mean by that?"

"Well," Miss Caverill said, fidgeting a trifle in her seat, "it wasn't proper for a woman her age to paint herself up the way she did, rouge and all, and I am sure she took one too many more often than not."

"How do you know?"

"Well, why wouldn't I know? She was always in bed until late in the morning. She nearly always was asleep until I came to do her room. She really was a sight then, I must say. Her eyes were bloodshot and swollen like, and she was quite unsteady, and there was no doubt that she smelt of whisky."

"Did you know if Mr Murray and she were friendly? Did Mrs Blaine have occasion to say anything in your hearing concerning Mr Murray?"

"No, I am afraid not. I don't recall her say anything about Mr Murray at all."

"Well, thank you. That will be all, Miss Caverill," the Chief Inspector said, rising. He turned to Detective Sergeant Holmes and said, "Have you located Mr Soames?"

"Yes, sir, we have him right here."

Seeing my surprise at the mention of this unfamiliar name, the Chief Inspector smiled and said, "Your description of the man you said you bumped into whilst leaving Mr Murray's room fits a Mr Soames, who lives here. He was out when we enquired this morning, but he's back now."

A thin, short, harassed-looking man with an incongruous Charlie Chaplin moustache came in. This Mr Soames was the man I had bumped into, all right. He had the sort of appearance which made him easy to describe – especially the moustache – and the police must not have had much trouble locating him. Mrs Bleakely must have been able to give his name at once from the description I had given the police.

After Mr Soames had taken a seat, the Chief Inspector said, "Can you tell us if you remember bumping into a gentleman last evening when you were coming in at the front door?"

"Eh? Er ... I am afraid I don't understand." Mr Soames's perplexity was comical.

A slight smile crossed the Chief Inspector's face, and he explained the purpose of the interview.

Mr Soames remembered then and recognised me. He was also able to confirm that Don had been with me at the time of the incident.

The Chief Inspector rose and gave me a mischievous smile. "Well, things are looking up," he said. "At least we have one suspect less to contend with now. I think."

"Thank you!" I said grinning. "That's a relief!"

The coroner's court met at nine thirty the next morning in a dingy building. The coroner was a scraggly man with pinched cheeks. He had false teeth that were loose, so his words came out with an irritating hiss. There were only a few persons present at the hearing. Celia had accompanied me and gave evidence of identification. Mrs Bleakely and Miss Caverill gave evidence and confirmed the factual details of finding the body. The medical evidence showed that death was due to carbon monoxide poisoning. The time of death was established as between nine and ten p.m. Evidence from the laboratory analysis showed that there was some barbiturate derivative in the deceased's stomach. The coroner wasted no time in eliciting the information and carried out his enquiries briskly and precisely. The atmosphere, despite the gravity of the situation, was informal and quite relaxed. The police asked for an adjournment, as had been anticipated, and this was granted.

Having finished with the ordeal of the inquest, Celia now had the funeral to face. Mrs Haversham was able to make arrangements with her church to have a service and for the body to be cremated in the church's own crematorium. I placed an advertisement in the *Times* and personally contacted some of Don and Celia's closest friends about the arrangements. Altogether, about seventy-five people were present at the funeral service. Celia and I sat with Mr and Mrs Haversham in the front pew, our eyes drawn irresistibly to the coffin before the altar. The priest, a young man in his early thirties, made a brief, emotional sermon about Don's untimely death and drew from it the moral that because death comes unannounced, like a thief in the night, we must all be in readiness at all times to meet it, without fear of what we may otherwise have to contend with as punishment for our sins in the hereafter – a theological truth that apparently left only an ephemeral impact on most of the congregation, judging from their bored faces.

Celia had agreed with the suggestion of Mrs Haversham's that the ashes be interred in Wimbledon as soon as possible after they had been handed over. Celia had them that very evening, and she and I took the urn with Don's ashes to Wimbledon the next day and had it interred in the cemetery only a mile from Craven Manor. A cold wind blew through the cemetery, lifting the edges of the attendees' coats, ruffling their hair, shaking the branches of the bordering trees, and whistling eerily through the leaves. The unpleasant weather and the wind added to the grimness of the occasion. Mr and Mrs Haversham did not attend, as it was too tiring for them. However, many of Celia and Don's friends in Wimbledon, some of whom had not been able to attend the church service in London, were present, as were a few of the education and church staff in London who had worked with Don. The urn with Don's ashes was confined to a small grave after a brief ceremony, which included the ritual readings of the Anglican service for the dead and a few standard hymns. Celia bore it all with fortitude, but the depth of her anguish was clear from the deep furrows that sadness had brought to her brow. It was, indeed, a sad moment for all of us who had known and loved Don, whose liveliness and charm had endeared himself to everyone and who was, therefore, sincerely missed.

Chapter 10

I had returned to London the day after the funeral service and spent the night at my hotel, the Prince Edward, at Marble Arch. I had woken up rather late, taken a cold shower, and was about to ring room service for my breakfast when the phone rang.

I picked it up. "Good morning, sir. This is reception. There is a Sergeant Holmes here to see you. Shall I send him up, or would you prefer to see him in the lounge?"

I didn't like the idea of being detained in my room on what appeared from my window to be a lovely, sunny morning. "I'll see him in the lounge," I said. "Will you please ask him to wait? I shall be down presently."

I wondered what Detective Sergeant Holmes wanted with me. I decided I'd have my breakfast later. I couldn't imagine what it was all about, and although I was a trifle annoyed at his turning up when he did, I was anxious to know whether the police enquiry into Don's death had progressed.

When I went down, Detective Sergeant Holmes and another man whom I recognised as one of the constables were seated in the lounge. They got up from their seats on seeing me and came forward. They were both in plain clothes.

"Good morning, sir," the Detective Sergeant said as he shook my hand. "Sorry to disturb you this lovely morning, but it's important that you come down to the Yard with us."

He was a genial sort, with a bright, good-natured smile. "We have located Miss Hamilton, and the Chief Inspector would like you to identify her."

I told him that I would report to the Chief Inspector as soon as I had had my breakfast. The Detective Sergeant requested that I not delay, as the Chief Inspector had an appointment later in the day, and he and the constable left.

When I arrived at Chief Inspector Smith's office at Scotland Yard, I found him seated at his desk conversing with a young woman who sat directly opposite him. I could not see her face at first, but she turned her head in my direction when the Chief Inspector greeted me, and I got a glimpse of a strikingly beautiful face. I was wondering who she could be when the Chief Inspector rose and said, half to the lady, "Ah, Mr Benison, we have Miss Hamilton with us. You have met before, I believe."

I was baffled. I could see a similar expression on the lady's face.

"No," I said. "We haven't met before."

"I haven't set eyes on him in all my life," she said, as if to confirm my statement.

"There seems to be some error, then," the Chief Inspector said. "I had the impression that you two had already met."

"There has been some error, indeed," I said. "The lady I met who called herself Ada Hamilton was quite a different person."

I could see why Don had been so lavish in his praise of Miss Hamilton, if indeed, this was she. She was an incontestably beautiful woman. She had dark, limpid eyes; a small, straight nose; and full, sensuously chiselled lips on a delicately oval face. She had a rich suntanned complexion and a neat, provocative figure. Her general appearance was smart and projected a certain feline grace which was arresting. She had an air about her which gave one the impression of gentility and elegance. She certainly didn't look the common tramp she really was. It would have been quite easy to be deceived by her, as Don had no doubt been.

The woman I had met at Celia's was hardly like Miss Hamilton. If one were to describe them generally, though, perhaps there were certain points of resemblance.

They both were dark complexioned, with dark hair and eyes, and decidedly foreign, possibly from the same or related ethnic groups. But a more specific comparison stripped them of any resemblance whatsoever. The real Ada Hamilton looked beautiful and refined, whereas the woman I had met at Celia's had been rather pretty in a coarse sort of way, and her deportment and dress could not have suggested refinement in any way. Miss Hamilton was decidedly a woman of the world. She was poised and well groomed, and she gave the impression of being self-assured and knowing, whereas the other woman had seemed frightened and diffident. Miss Hamilton was a good three inches taller and full-chested whereas the other possessed the kind of slenderness that bordered on thinness and gave the impression of being fragile.

"Miss Hamilton," said the Chief Inspector, "I should explain why Mr Benison is here." He briefly and clearly recounted the story of the woman who had approached Celia and whom I had had occasion to meet. "Do you have any idea who this woman is who called herself by your name?"

"I haven't the slightest notion," she said.

"Miss Hamilton," the Chief Inspector said with asperity, "the woman who visited Mrs Murray knew of your connection with Mr Murray – she knew even as much to state that she was to have Mr Murray's child, and she was in possession of letters written by Mr Murray to you." The Chief Inspector paused ominously. "And what's more, from all accounts she was a foreigner whose description closely fits that of a woman of your own country. Really, it is too much for you to pretend that you know nothing of this woman."

"It is possible that this woman who impersonated me got hold of my letters from Mr Murray and decided to use them for blackmail," Miss Hamilton said.

"From Mr Murray?" the Chief Inspector said incredulously. "Those were letters written to you, Miss

Hamilton, by Mr Murray. Only you could have been in possession of them."

"Actually, Chief Inspector, there were some letters of mine in Mr Murray's possession. It happened like this: Just before we broke up, Mr Murray and I had rather a showdown at my flat."

Miss Hamilton uncrossed her legs and, leaning forward in her chair, continued. "You see, I was very much in love with him, and when he threatened to have nothing more to do with me, I told him that I could ruin his marriage and his career by making his letters public. He demanded that I give them to him. When I refused, he ransacked my dressing table and found some of the letters he had written, which I had kept in an envelope in one of the drawers. There were others and I told him that I had well hidden those, and he was furious. He tried to make me give them to him, but I wouldn't. They were the more recent ones. I had kept them in my jacket pocket and forgotten to take them out. I later found them. I didn't think there was any point in my keeping them, so I tore them up sometime afterwards. As I said, this woman who visited Mrs Murray could have got hold of the letters Mr Murray took and used them. She could have taken my name from the letters to pretend she was me."

"Did you know if Mr Murray knew any other woman?"

"It is quite likely that he may have after he left me. How was I to know?"

Don had told me about the incident in which he had taken the letters back from Miss Hamilton and had said that he was aware that some of them might still be in her possession. But Miss Hamilton's suggestion that some other woman could have got hold of them seemed far-fetched. And I felt quite certain that Don didn't have dealings with any other young woman. But, of course, on an objective appraisal of the situation, I could not dismiss the possibility that Don may have had relations with other women and that they could have visited his room and got the letters. Besides, I had earlier gathered from the Chief Inspector that the police had not discovered any letters among Don's possessions. Although Don would most likely have destroyed them, theoretically at least, one could not discount the possibility that someone had taken them.

"Miss Hamilton," the Chief Inspector said, "did you write any letters to Mr Murray?"

"No, I did not. Mr Murray used to joke about it. I didn't think there was any need to write since I met him quite often, and in any case, I am a very bad correspondent."

"Yes, but whoever this other woman was knew that you were supposedly pregnant. How do you explain that she knew that, Miss Hamilton?"

"I don't know," she said. "Oh, but I did send him a note a couple of weeks back asking him to come and see me and telling him that I had not lied when I had told him that I was carrying his child."

The Chief Inspector said, "When did you last meet Mr Murray?"

"About eight weeks ago."

"Was it on that occasion that he informed you that he was breaking off his relations with you?"

"Yes."

"What made him break it off with you?"

Miss Hamilton cleared her throat, lifted her head, and looked away. "He said that he no longer loved me."

"Was there any reason for this sudden pronouncement on his part? It was sudden, I take it?"

"I don't know why. I suppose he must have tired of me."

"Didn't he tell you why? Come, come, Miss Hamilton, let's have the truth," the Chief Inspector said sternly. "Wasn't it because he had discovered who you really were – that you weren't the lady you pretended to be, but a woman of the streets?"

Miss Hamilton bowed her head and stared somewhat defiantly at the floor but said nothing.

"Did you communicate with Mr Murray after his final visit to your flat?"

"Yes, only to ring him up and tell him I was pregnant. But he wouldn't believe me, and that was why I also sent him the note."

There was a pause, and the Chief Inspector said, "Are you with child, Miss Hamilton?"

Miss Hamilton heaved a sigh and shook her head. "No. I thought that would bring him back to me."

"Miss Hamilton," the Chief Inspector said, "we would like you to give us an account of your movements on the evening of sixteenth July – the evening, that is, of Mr Murray's death."

Miss Hamilton crossed her slim, shapely legs. Her bearing was composed and revealed no sign of agitation.

"Well," she began, "there wasn't much that I did that evening. I spent the afternoon in bed after having taken some aspirins. I had caught the flu and felt feverish and unwell. So I decided to stay indoors. Around four thirty in the evening, I went down to the chemist across the street to buy some throat lozenges. After I returned, I wasn't feeling any better, so I locked myself in my room and stayed in bed with a book. At about eight p.m. when I was just thinking of making my dinner and a hot drink, I heard the telephone ring. When I picked it up, I was quite surprised to hear Mr Murray's voice."

"Surprised?"

"Yes, surprised. Mr Murray had made it quite plain that everything was over between us. Naturally, I didn't ever expect to hear from him."

"Please continue."

"Well, he was ever so nice over the phone. He said that he was sorry for having treated me the way he had and asked if I was free to come over to his hotel. I told him that I was ill but would drop in the following day."

Miss Hamilton drew out a handkerchief from her handbag and gently dabbed the shine off her nose. "That didn't seem to satisfy him. He seemed rather anxious to see me right away. He asked if he could come over to mine, but I put him off by saying that I really wasn't feeling like seeing anybody and was going to bed. I told him I'd see him first thing the following morning, which was a Sunday, and he said that would be fine."

"Didn't he mention anything else to you? Nothing about what he had thought was your visit to see Mrs Murray?"

"No. We spoke about nothing more than I have already told you."

The Chief Inspector remained silent for a while, as if pondering the whole thing, and then he addressed Miss Hamilton again. "From your statement, I take it that, except for your visit to the chemist, you were unwell and spent your evening alone in your room. Isn't that so?"

"Yes. That is so," she said decisively.

"Is there anyone who may have noticed your movements and who may be able to support your statement – the landlady, your immediate neighbours, anyone at all?"

"I am afraid I don't think so."

The Chief Inspector got up from his seat. "Thank you, Miss Hamilton. That will be all for now. We should like to record your statement. The Detective Sergeant here will attend to you."

I watched her as she walked sedately into the next room, with the burly Detective Sergeant leading the way. She carried herself erect, and her clothes stretched tightly over her body, accentuating the roundness of her hips and the smallness of her waist. She was svelte.

"What do you think?" the Chief Inspector said when we were alone.

"All this business about someone having taken the letters from Don and used them to extort money from

Celia doesn't make sense," I said. "In the first place, why should anyone want to show Don's letters to his wife? It was Don who should have been blackmailed, with the threat of exposing his affair to his wife. Surely if money were the motive, that would have been the sensible thing to do, not to go directly to his wife and ask her for money."

The Chief Inspector grunted and said, "That is all very fine, but someone did go to Mrs Murray, and she did request money. So there you are."

"It could be, of course, that Miss Hamilton was trying to get back at Don by exposing him to his wife, whilst also making some money from the deal," I suggested.

The Chief Inspector pondered this awhile. "On the other hand," he mused, "if Miss Hamilton's story is true and some other woman was involved, then it would make sense that such a person could not have blackmailed Mr Murray with Miss Hamilton's letters, although she could have tried to obtain money from his wife on the pretext of being Miss Hamilton."

"I see what you mean," I said, "but whoever concocted such a scheme must have a terribly warped mind to think she had a chance extorting funds from a man's wife for what he had done. She must have been desperate or just plain crazy. Although, mind you, the plan nearly worked."

The Chief Inspector was silent a bit, as if trying to come to grips with this conundrum. "We can be sure of nothing," he said, "until we first find out who this other woman was."

"Even if there is any connection between that woman and the real Miss Hamilton, it doesn't seem reasonable that Miss

Hamilton would have been responsible for Don's death if her intention had been to extort money from him. His being killed has certainly put paid to all that."

"Hmm," the Chief Inspector said meditatively. "You could be right there, but Miss Hamilton's motive may have been pure vengeance. A woman scorned, and all that. Women are unpredictable creatures, and I have seen enough queer happenings in my time to know that anything is possible."

Before I took my leave of the Chief Inspector, he wished to know what my plans were. I had decided to stay on for a few more days in London and settle some of my affairs. Besides, I felt that it would be necessary for me to stay on awhile for Celia's sake as well. I hadn't yet discovered what her plans were, but it was very unlikely that she would want to go back to her house in Wimbledon just yet.

Chapter 11

I took a taxi to my hotel. It was still early, so I decided I'd go and see Celia after helping myself to a beer at the hotel lounge.

It was a lovely afternoon, so I chose to take a bus to Shepherd's Bush instead of a taxi. It had been some time since I'd boarded a bus, and the prospect of sitting in the top deck of a double-decker on such a bright, sunny day seemed exciting.

When I reached my destination, it was around teatime. Celia's uncle, Mr Haversham, let me in. He was an old man with silvery hair and heavily pouched eyes. He wore a short-sleeved khaki shirt and baggy grey trousers belted at the waist. He was a jolly man normally, with a bright twinkle in his eyes, but he let me in solemnly, clearly saddened by his concern for Celia.

He motioned me to a chair and puffed at a shabby pipe, peering ruminatively at the wall.

Before I could ask him, he said, removing his pipe, "She's not in. She and Ruth have gone to church. It was Ruth's idea. She felt a chat with the vicar might do Celia good, you know. The poor girl's gone to pieces."

I asked, "Is she very upset?"

"I'd say she is," Mr Haversham said, keeping his pipe in his teeth and speaking from the corner of his mouth. "She won't eat a thing and locks herself up in her room most of the time. It's a wonder she consented to go out."

As it was unlikely that Celia would be back for quite a while, and as I was hungry, I told Mr Haversham that I would drop in again soon and took my leave.

I did see Celia a couple of days later, quite by accident, although I did not get a chance to talk to her. I was returning to my hotel around five thirty p.m. after a shopping spree and got off the Tube at Marble Arch. I had barely emerged onto the street when, to my surprise and delight, I saw Celia not fifty yards away talking intently to another woman in the shadow of a tobacconist's shop. The woman she was talking to had a gaunt, sharp face and wore a scarf round her head. She had weather-beaten skin, and it was obvious that she was not of the class of people Celia normally associated with. She was probably someone Celia had met casually and engaged with in a polite conversation, as she was wont to do at times. Before I could hail her, however, Celia and the woman walked briskly towards the stairway down to the Tube at the further end and were soon out of sight. For a moment I thought of following them and calling out to Celia, but I soon lost sight of them in the heavy after-work crowd that was just beginning to fill the Tube station.

Afterwards, I busied myself with some of my private affairs. I had business in the City, a few things to attend to, and some shopping to get done. There is something in the atmosphere of London which makes me bustle about with activity and enthusiasm. It was early August and the sun was shining. Life was brimming over so that one felt jostled into keeping pace with it. At Wimbledon I spent a great deal of my time at home, punctuated only with the occasional quiet stroll or visits to the club and friends'; but life here, walking the streets and peering into the shops and mingling with the ceaseless flow of humanity, kept me active and agile.

For three days after Don's funeral, I had lost myself in the myriad interests of London. Don's loss and the circumstances of his death had affected me deeply, and my mind sought to free itself from the gloom and distress that pervaded it.

I twice visited Celia, but there wasn't much I was able to say to her, and I felt that she preferred to be left alone. It was only natural that her grief so soon after Don's death should overwhelm her and that she should feel so disinclined to resume the normal activities of life.

One afternoon I was returning to the hotel after a pleasant stroll in the park when I noticed Chief Inspector Smith's burly figure leaving the hotel lounge. I had crossed the road and stepped onto the pavement in front of the hotel when he saw me, and his face lit up with a smile.

"Hello," he said cheerfully as though pleasantly surprised. "I've been waiting for you in the lounge for over twenty minutes and was just leaving. How very fortunate that I should bump into you."

We shook hands. He was a pleasant fellow, and I was beginning to like him.

"Well," I said, "it is a stroke of luck. I am hardly ever in. Spend most of my time exploring London. Do come in." I led the way to the lounge, and we settled ourselves comfortably.

"Well, what brings you here?" I said. "Business as usual, no doubt, but first let's enjoy a drink and warm our insides, shall we?"

I motioned to a waiter who had already started to approach our table.

"You're not on duty until you've had a drink," I said genially, and the Chief Inspector laughed. "What'll it be?"

"Oh, anything at all. Whatever you have," he said.

I ordered two whiskies and sodas.

"Has anything cropped up?" I asked.

The waiter brought us our drinks.

"Well, yes. There are a few developments that I thought might interest you. We checked out Miss Hamilton's story and came up with rather a lot of useful information."

"Go on," I said, "tell me all. I am awfully eager to know. I felt, of course, that Miss Hamilton's story didn't quite hold together, but she seemed so sure and convincing that it was difficult not to have been taken in by her."

"It's always so with the pathological liar," the Chief Inspector said expansively. "One comes across the type so frequently in our work. All antisocial types are natural liars. It becomes a necessity in order to conceal their deviant activities. It is second nature to them, and they quite often lie where no deception is necessary; it becomes a sort of compulsion. Anyway, when we checked Miss Hamilton's bona fides, we came across a host of lies." The Chief Inspector lit a cigarette and puffed out a cloud of smoke. I summoned a nearby waiter and ordered another round of drinks.

"Tell me, Chief Inspector," I said facetiously, "what web of falsehood has she spun, and what have you discovered?"

"To begin with," he said, "she told us that she had not gone to Mr Murray's room that night, but she had."

"But how could you know?" I queried incredulously. "Did someone see her?"

"Yes. The taxi driver did," the Chief Inspector said with a twinkle in his eye.

My face must have shown puzzlement, for the Chief Inspector explained, "We checked out her story. The chemist remembers her coming in at about the time she mentions. There is no reason to doubt that she didn't have her dinner out; it is quite likely that she ate at home. But she did go out around nine o'clock that evening by taxi. We did a routine check of taxi drivers working in the locality on spec and asked them if they remembered picking up a woman of Miss Hamilton's description around the specified time. Miss Hamilton being an exceptionally striking woman and a foreigner to boot, we reckoned that if she had gone out in a taxi, we'd hear about it. We questioned a number of drivers, and sure enough, one of them said he remembered picking up a young lady of very similar description not far from where Miss Hamilton lives. He dropped her off some little distance away from the Clarendon hotel. He said he remembered her quite well. He also noticed that she spoke with a foreign accent and that she had worn a leopard-skin cape. He said he would be able to identify her."

"That was pretty good luck, wasn't it? After all, she could have taken a bus or even the Underground. You were lucky she took a taxi."

"Very lucky, indeed. But we were fairly confident that if she had gone to visit Mr Murray, she would have gone by taxi, as, being a prostitute, it would have been more or less habitual for her to travel that way. It's the generally accepted mode of travel in her trade, especially at night, for obvious reasons."

The Chief Inspector paused and coughed into his handkerchief. "Well," he said, replacing his handkerchief in his coat pocket, "we brought her in and held an identification parade. The cabbie picked her out, all right. A search of her apartment also revealed the leopard-skin cape. At first she denied having gone anywhere, but when she saw that the evidence of the identification parade was quite conclusive, she admitted to having paid a visit to Mr Murray's room that night. She reiterated that Mr Murray had rung her up around eight and pleaded with her to come and see him. He said that he was sorry for the way he had treated her and that he would put everything right and that he wanted to sort things out between them. She said he made no mention over the phone of her supposed visit to Mrs Murray's in Wimbledon. She said she was glad at the prospect of meeting Mr Murray again after what had seemed an irrevocable rift. Nevertheless, she was feeling very ill and told him she could see him only on the following morning. But around eight thirty, she felt better and decided she would go and see him after all. She thought she would surprise him. She was sure he would be in because he didn't generally go out in the evenings, as he enjoyed imbibing a few whiskies in his room late into the night. She had, therefore, washed, changed clothes, and taken a taxi to his hotel."

"And did she see him?" I asked with the air of a man who would take anything she said with a pinch of salt.

"Yes, she says she did," the Chief Inspector said curtly, "but according to her, he was already dead by then."

"Come, come," I said, "we are not supposed to believe such balderdash, are we? A smart piece of thinking on her part, I must say. But the time of her visit does more or less coincide with the time of Mr Murray's death as given by the coroner, doesn't it?"

"It does. Mr Murray's death has, as you know, been established at between nine and ten p.m.," the Chief Inspector said. "That together with the mendacity of her original statement makes one very suspicious indeed. But, of course, her explanation is that she refrained from mentioning her visit to Mr Murray in her first statement precisely because she felt that she might be suspected of his murder, as no one would believe that she had only chanced upon his dead body. We are holding her in custody, though, pending bail."

"How did she gain entrance to the hotel?" I asked. "Either Don or someone else must have opened the door for her."

"If you remember, the front door lock is broken and anybody can enter the premises by merely pushing open the door. Miss Hamilton says that having entered the hotel in this way, she knocked on Mr Murray's door but got no reply. She thought that he may have left his room momentarily, so, knowing that he kept his door key above the door, she fetched it and opened the door. She says that she was immediately conscious of a strong odour. The room was dark, but she found the switch on the wall and put the light on. She was shocked by what she saw. She tried to wake him up but quickly realised that he was dead. Thereafter, she says that she was seized with panic and switched off the light and fled from the room."

The Chief Inspector heaved in a sigh and pushed out his chest and prepared to get up from his seat. "But, that is just her story and there is nothing to support it. The evidence against her is naturally very strong. She had a motive for murdering Mr Murray, love turned sour, you know. She was at the scene of the crime at approximately the time of the deceased's death, a fact which she tried to conceal by making a false statement to the police. And, there is no evidence at all to indicate who else may have done it."

The Chief Inspector now made towards the door, his felt hat in his hand. "There is, however, one matter which needs clearing up if we are to present a smooth case, and that is who the woman was who visited Mrs Murray. It is quite likely that Ada Hamilton had an accomplice, but to what purpose, I cannot quite imagine."

"Incidentally," I said, "I take it that Miss Hamilton also confessed to having closed the gas tap and that there is no more mystery about that now?"

"On the contrary," the Chief Inspector said. "She quite categorically denies having had anything to do with the gas tap. Either she is telling the truth or she just doesn't want us to think she had anything to do with it."

"That would be it, surely," I said. "After all, her admission arose from the fact that there was evidence of her visit to see Don. Her saying that he was already dead then can only be her way of wriggling out of the mess she has got herself into. The obvious presumption is that she killed Don by gassing him. Therefore, she must have opened the tap, and although she hasn't confessed to closing it, we have no alternative but to presume that she must have done. Maybe she panicked and lost her presence of mind."

"Well," the Chief Inspector said, bowing as we shook hands on his way out. "That, as you say, is what we have to find out, and find out we shall, I am sure. Good day."

Chapter 12

I was standing at the open window of my third-floor apartment and looking down at the street, watching the spectacle of traffic and human beings moving along. There weren't many people about, it being about six thirty p.m. on a Sunday. Couples walked languidly in the sun. Some of the men had removed their jackets and carried them either slung over their shoulders or on their arms. The women wore bright coloured cotton clothes as befitting a summer's day. It was peaceful to watch this array of human beings on such a sultry, sun-washed day. I let my eyes rove up and down the street in a kind of languid trance, whilst my mind, drowsy with the glare and the heat, barely registered any thought and seemed nearly to have stopped functioning. I must have been in this delightful state of inertia for a few minutes when my mind was jolted into life again. A woman was approaching from down the street whom I could have sworn was Celia. Although her face was unrecognisable from where I was, there was that unmistakable grace that was part and parcel of Celia, and I had no doubts that it was her. As the figure approached and her face became recognisable, I shouted out her name, my voice sharp with the excitement of having seen her so unexpectedly.

I waved as I shouted. She heard and raised her head to locate the origin of the sound. I leaned half out of the window and kept waving, and then I noticed something strange. At sight of me, a man who was only a few yards behind Celia turned his head sharply to the side and covered his face with a handkerchief. It was only a momentary act, but it struck me beyond doubt that the man was eager to conceal his face from me. In the meantime, Celia had spotted me and waved back and smiled, pointing towards my room and indicating with a gesture that she was going to come up.

"Wait down in the lounge," I called. "I shall join you in a minute."

I noticed that the man behind Celia pulled his hat over his face and walked directly under my window. He wore a grey suit and was of middle height and a stocky build. I had the feeling that he had been following Celia, but it seemed such a ridiculous notion that I gave it no further thought.

It was nice to see Celia up and about after what seemed such a long time. Don's death had cast such a gloom on her mind that she had refused to venture out on her own and had incarcerated herself. It was nice to see her look more like her normal self again.

Celia was waiting in the lounge when I arrived. She wore a white dress that had the palest mauve flowers on it. She smiled and rose from the settee on seeing me. She looked charming. She seemed as young and as lovely as when I had known her in the days before Don had taken her to be his wife, as in those long-forgotten days when I had loved her and she had been dear to me. Seeing her like this, alone and unprotected, I felt stirring within me some inexplicable longing, some awakening of a bygone and long-subdued emotion. I held her outstretched hands.

"It is good to see you, Celia," I said.

Her eyes looked softly into mine. "It is nice to see you too," she said, her fingers gripping mine tightly.

"Shall we go up to my room? Let's use the stairs," I said, leading the way. "It's only a few flights up." We reached my room a trifle breathless but elated.

"Will you have a drink?"

"Yes. I'd like a beer, please, if it's no bother," Celia said, seating herself and still panting a little after the climb.

"No bother at all," I said. "I always keep a few bottles handy in the fridge."

I poured out the drinks, handed Celia her glass, and sat down on the only remaining chair in the room. We sipped our drinks for a while, saying nothing. Somehow it was suddenly difficult to make conversation. The memory of Don's death still hung over us like a dark cloud that obscured everything else. Some diversion and an atmosphere more conducive to distraction was what was necessary, and I decided that it would be best if we left my room and went out for a while.

"Come, my dear," I said. "Sitting here isn't going to do us any good. Let's go for a stroll, shall we?"

"Oh, yes," Celia said. "I would like that."

Having gulped down our drinks, we left the hotel and stepped onto the street. The evening was young and we walked aimlessly and peered into the shop windows, stopping every now and again to look at something that caught our fancy. It was pleasant to be out mingling with the crowd, who, like ourselves, seemed to be ambling along, in and out of the cafes and shops. After we had been walking for quite a while, I was beginning to feel the need for something to eat. The time had passed quickly; it was already eight thirty p.m. and the evening was waning into night.

"Hungry?" I asked Celia.

"Starving," she replied with a smile. "This heat does give one an appetite."

The gloom had somewhat lifted, and I held Celia's hand in mine, feeling like a boy again.

"You choose the place," I said.

"I know just the job," Celia said, her voice now excited at the prospect of good food. "A little Indian restaurant off Tottenham Court Road called the Alfatha. They serve the most delicious curries there."

"Then the Alfatha it shall be," I said exuberantly.

We were on Oxford Street, but we decided to walk the distance instead of taking the Oxford Circus Tube. Celia put her hand on my arm, and I clasped her fingers with my own and we smiled at each other. A rakish happiness had engulfed me. I hadn't felt so cheerful and young at heart for a long time.

The Alfatha proved to be a charming little place. It was situated in a basement, so we had to walk down a flight of narrow steps and then enter through a narrow door. The floor was carpeted with some glossy red material and the decor was a trifle garish but quaintly South Asian and exotic. Soft Hindi music crooned over the radio, and a turbaned Indian waiter escorted us gravely to the only vacant table at the end of the hall.

We had a most delectable meal, starting with glasses of Madeira and ending with Turkish coffee. Both Celia and I had quite a penchant for hot Indian cuisine, and the chapattis and Madras curried beef had been most satisfying and filling.

Celia chatted gaily and irrepressibly, but at times I felt that she kept talking more as a means of liberating her mind from anguish than as an expression of gaiety. But she seemed happy enough, and I was pleased to see her more like herself again.

It is strange how the mind can experience anew sensations which had seemed dead and forgotten. It was true that I had loved Celia not so very long ago, but since her marriage to Don, my mind had adjusted to the circumstance and time had reduced the flame until there seemed hardly an ember left. But seeing her now alone and unhappy awakened a strong response within me, and once again something like the old yearning seemed to have laid hold of my heart. It was as if the in-between years had never been, as if the mind and the heart had never aged but remained still young, vulnerable, and free. Tracing our way back along Tottenham Court Road, satiated after a good dinner, we walked arm in arm and in silence. It was one of those moments of inner harmony, when the souls touch, and when silence is far more eloquent than words. As we rounded a corner, the elegiac strains of a violin wafted towards us from somewhere across the street, sweet and low.

"Let's listen awhile," said Celia, pressing my arm gently. We crossed the road to where a small group of men and women stood in an arcade in front of a shop window. Peering through the crowd, we saw a young man with a mop of dishevelled hair seated by a pillar, playing solemnly on his instrument. On a wooden stand stood a notice which read, "Please help student collect funds for furthering art studies." The young man wore a soiled grey coat and brown corduroy trousers. His cap containing his collections lay on the ground midway between the crowd and himself.

The dulcet notes of the violin and their melancholy strain filled the mind with a strange nostalgia and quaint sadness, which elevated the soul.

I watched Celia as she looked at the artist, but I saw that her eyes saw nothing; they were like the eyes of the blind. I watched her as if hypnotised.

"Celia," I said gently to break the spell.

She turned her eyes to me with the puzzlement of one who had suddenly emerged from a dream. "I'm sorry," she said, affecting a smile. "I must have been dreaming."

"You were," I said gently, and took her arm. We walked awhile without saying anything until Celia said with a sudden desperate intensity in her voice, "Ben, you will always stand by me, won't you? I feel so alone, so lost and afraid."

In an instant, she took my face in her hands and drew it to hers. We kissed, and Celia clung to me and buried her face in my chest.

From then on I spent most of my time with Celia. I was a regular visitor to the Havershams' home, and our days were spent almost entirely in outings and jaunts into the City. In this way we spent almost a fortnight, which passed away so rapidly in careless enjoyment that it seemed only a few days.

It was soon evident, however, that I could not continue in London indefinitely, as I had my work and other matters to attend to in Wimbledon. I had already long overstayed my sojourn.

Celia, too, had to return to Craven Manor, no longer a home but a house, although it was her rightful abode of which she was mistress. She explained to me that at first the thought of going back to that house, now desolate without Don, had been very daunting and depressing to her; so depressing that she was unable to even contemplate it, but gradually her mind had become accustomed to the notion, and she had set about making plans to return to it.

Chapter 13

We decided to make the journey together, and early on a Friday evening, having taken our leave of the Havershams, we boarded the train to Wimbledon. Prior to leaving, I had dropped in on the Chief Inspector to inform him of my departure, as he had requested. He was seated at his desk, peering over his spectacles at a file which lay open before him. He arose, smiling broadly, and motioned me to a chair.

"Well," I said taking a seat, "I promised to inform you before I left London, and here I am to do just that. Mrs Murray and I will be leaving for Wimbledon this evening."

"I'm glad you'll be around to take care of Mrs Murray," the Chief Inspector said. "I'm sure she'll need all the help she can get."

"Yes, I'm afraid the whole thing has knocked her over," I said. "By the way, have you had any further developments?"

"Nothing new, I'm afraid, but we do have our men on the job. Nothing as yet known about Mrs Blaine. There is something fishy about that woman disappearing like that on the very evening of the death."

"Well," I said, rising to leave, "I would appreciate it if you could keep me informed of any developments. Naturally, I would be most interested to know how the investigations are proceeding."

"I will most certainly keep you informed," the Chief Inspector said, accompanying me to the door. "Do please convey my regards to Mrs Murray, will you?"

I bade him goodbye and left.

When our train arrived at Wimbledon, it was getting to be twilight. We took a taxi from the station to Craven Manor. It was nice to be back at Wimbledon, which, after the noise and bustle of London, offered a soothing atmosphere of wide-openness and suburban quiet. It had been good to be in London, but one could not live there for too long, and I had been feeling the need for respite.

The taxi passed through the town and, veering left off the main road, turned into the driveway of Craven Manor.

The house's large gates and stately porch loomed bleakly against the darkening sky. The rhododendrons that skirted the wide lawn were laden with flowers at this season, it being the end of summer. It was a pleasant sight after the brown brick buildings of London. I paid the taxi driver at the door, having removed our luggage onto the doorstep, and rang the bell.

Old Mrs Feston, whom Celia had telephoned about our arrival, opened the door. She kissed Celia and tearfully clasped her hands, saying how happy she was to see her. She was visibly moved. Celia and I followed Mrs Feston inside, and Celia flung herself into a chair with a great sigh of relief. I put the bags in the hall, and Mrs Feston scampered away to bring us tea. Presently she returned with a tray laden with the teapot, two cups and saucers, and plates of freshly made scones and apple tarts still hot from the oven.

We helped ourselves greedily and gratefully sipped our tea. A thin drizzle had begun, and it appeared it would persist. The dusk was gathering noiselessly and the crickets were chirping on the lawn. "It's lovely to be back," Celia said softly, looking out of the window, her face an exquisite cameo against the evening light.

Yes, it was good to be back. I was glad that she had left London and come home when she did. Here she could find time to rest, to occupy herself, and to recuperate. I knew that her home had cheered her already.

Mrs Feston spoke of the lovely weather Wimbledon had been having and of other matters in general.

I was very tired and looking forward to bed, but I didn't want to leave Celia to herself so early, so when she asked me to stay for supper, I assented.

Supper was served a while later. Mrs Feston had lain the table and brought in the dishes. She hovered about serving what she had made before settling down to eat. It was nice to sit down to some home cooking after so many meals snatched in cafes and hotels.

When we had finished, Mrs Feston carried away the plates, and we moved into the sitting room. I lit my pipe and sat down, and Celia excused herself to help with the coffee. It was served soon after. When we had finished it, Mrs Feston took the cups away and bade us goodnight before retiring for the night.

Celia's body sank into the depths of the settee, and her legs stretched out in weary relaxation. She had removed her shoes for comfort and thrown her head back in an attitude of rest, but her eyes were wide open.

Celia said, quite out of the blue, "Ben, have they found any clues to Don's death?"

"Well … er … yes, I think they have," I said, a little taken aback by the question. It was the first time in weeks that Celia had mentioned anything at all in connection with Don, let alone the ugly subject of his death.

"Signs seems to indicate that Miss Hamilton had something to do with it. You see, the Chief Inspector has obtained quite irrefutable evidence that she did visit Don on the evening of his death. The taxi driver who took her to his hotel was able to identify her, and Miss Hamilton herself has since made an admission to that effect, revising her first statement that she didn't leave her room that night. However, she states that when she entered Don's room, he was already dead. Nobody's going to believe that, of course.

After all, what else could she say? I think it won't be long before they'll have her up for trial."

"Well, what's holding them up? There is hardly any doubt that she did it, is there?" Celia said.

"Not really," I said. "Except that the police must find Ada Hamilton's imposter, the woman whom we met in this house on the day of Don's death. As long as she remains unknown, there will always be the presumption that other people besides the real Ada may have had something to do with Don's death."

"And what of that woman who is supposed to have disappeared from the hotel that night? The newspapers made some mention of her sudden and mysterious departure from the hotel. Mrs Blithe's her name, isn't it?"

"Mrs Blaine," I said. "Yes, they haven't located her either. Although there's probably no connection at all between her disappearance and Don's death, it is also a matter which will need clearing up sooner or later."

"I wish the whole sordid affair were done and over with," Celia said. "I think I'll go to bed now, Ben, if you don't mind. I am awfully tired."

In Wimbledon life settled back into the old groove, except, of course, that the loneliness of my life had been filled with the radiance of love, and things could never be the same again.

The days passed by happily. Celia too had somewhat resumed normalcy. My presence was naturally a great consolation to her, and our love a source of immense strength at a time when her life appeared to be at its bleakest. Gradually, she shed the dark mantle of despair that had burdened her since her husband's death. The first sanguine indications of her rehabilitation came in the gradual resumption of her former cheerfulness. She talked and laughed more and more and seemed to be her practical, efficient self again. She took a fresh interest in the garden and the house itself.

For my part, I spent my evenings out with her. We planned to do different things each day, and we often went on long drives before dusk to return refreshed by the evening air in time for dinner, which we contrived to have more often than not at Celia's.

Returning to Craven Manor one evening, we drove over the bridge which ran over the railway tracks. As we were halfway across, a train came suddenly out of the tunnel, hooting loudly and puffing out thick clouds of smoke, giving us both a shock. Celia seemed depressed. She said it reminded her of the gruesome newspaper story of a woman who had flung herself under an oncoming train that had inspired Tolstoy to write *Anna Karenina.*

It was around ten when we returned. This night was one of those rare occasions when we had eaten out – at the Café Royale, a fine-dining restaurant in the City – and it was later than usual. Celia seemed taut and stressed after the drive over the bridge, and I decided to stay over for a cup of coffee to cheer her up. We hadn't been in the house more than a few minutes when the phone rang. Celia was busy in the kitchen.

"Can you answer it, Ben?" she said, coming for a moment to the kitchen door with a cup and saucer in one hand and a bowl of sugar in the other.

I picked up the receiver. I had hardly put it to my ear when a woman's voice came over it clear but subdued. "Is that you, Mrs Murray?" There was something coldly insidious in the tone in which it was spoken; it was a harsh, gruff voice which had a strange quality.

"Just a moment," I said, speaking for the first time, and I thought I heard a stifled sound at the other end, which gave me the impression that the speaker had been surprised to hear a voice other than Celia's.

"It's for you," I called out to Celia, placing the receiver on the table.

"For me?" Celia said, perplexed. "Who on earth could it be and at this hour?"

She came over wiping her hands on her apron and picked up the receiver. "Hello," she called. "Hello? Hello?" Then she turned to me and said, her face suddenly a trifle pale, "There's no reply. I distinctively heard whoever it was ring off."

Celia walked away from the phone and came towards me.

"What could it mean?" Celia said. "I know he was listening while I talked, and I heard him deliberately drop the receiver."

"It wasn't a he," I said. "It was a she, I am sure, though it was a pretty gruff voice for a woman. I certainly haven't heard her voice before."

"Did she ask for me?"

"Yes," I said, "she said she wanted to speak to Mrs Murray."

There was, indeed, something odd about the incident. I could see that it had upset Celia. It was altogether a baffling episode, and although I tried to joke it off, neither of us could quite shed that sense of something faintly sinister for a while.

"It was probably some misunderstanding," I said. "Perhaps the woman didn't quite hear me, or perhaps she was in some sort of a hurry and had to drop the receiver without ceremony as she did."

"Perhaps," Celia said. "Perhaps there is some simple explanation after all."

Chapter 14

I was up to my neck with work in my office a little before noon when Chief Inspector Smith called. He was ringing from his office in London. After the preliminary salutations, he said, "We have located your imposter for you." Before I could quite fathom what he meant, he added, "She's a relative of Miss Hamilton's, and according to her statement, she was sent to see Mrs Murray by Miss Hamilton herself. Her name's Charlotte, Charlotte Polycarpou."

I caught on to what he was saying. "That's splendid," I said, "but how did you find her?"

"In our enquiries, we got to know that Miss Hamilton had shared a room for a few days a couple of years back with a compatriot of hers. The landlady's description of the woman seemed to fit in rather well with the one you gave us, and we made every effort to locate her whereabouts.

Naturally, at first we suspected that she, too, would be in the same profession as Miss Hamilton, but I'm afraid we were on the wrong track. Miss Polycarpou is not a prostitute. She is a student nurse, attached to St Mary's Hospital in Paddington. We chanced upon her. One of our boys detailed to shadow Miss Hamilton saw her go into St Mary's one day. He followed her and secretly watched her movements. Miss Hamilton delivered a message through one of the porters, and a while later, a young woman, obviously a foreigner, led Miss Hamilton rather furtively away to one of the interior rooms. Our man had a good description of the young lady who came to see Mrs Murray at Wimbledon, and after Miss Hamilton left, he questioned the young woman, who then gave him her name and relationship to Miss Hamilton. When she accompanied him to the police station, she decided after a while to tell the truth, and we have her confession."

"I suppose I'll have to come down to formally confirm her identity," I said.

"Yes, and Mrs Murray should as well, if she feels up to it. But she doesn't have to. Could you come in around eleven tomorrow morning?"

"Yes," I said, "I think I could drop in around that time. But I don't think Mrs Murray will feel up to it just now. By the way, what is her story? You haven't told me what explanation she offered for impersonating Miss Hamilton."

"Well, it's a bit of a long story. It appears that Miss Polycarpou, besides being a compatriot of Miss Hamilton's, is also her cousin. Apparently her mother was seriously ill – tumour of the brain – and the doctors had advised that she be flown over from Malta to America or England for an immediate operation. Miss Polycarpou had tried raising the money but couldn't get such a large sum as was required – £5,000 – at short notice and had sought the help of her cousin in this matter. Miss Hamilton then thought up the diabolical scheme of sending Miss Polycarpou to give Mrs Murray an ultimatum to obtain the money. Miss Hamilton had apparently known that Mr Murray had no money on him and that Celia held the reins over their bank account. Mr Murray is supposed to have told Miss Hamilton so when she had tried to get money from him on the pretext that she was going to have his child. So, she thought of intimidating Mrs Murray to get her to pay up. It's more likely, I think, that her scheme was an act of pure spite and that she didn't in the least expect Mrs Murray to fork over the money."

"But why didn't Miss Hamilton come for the money herself instead of sending Miss Polycarpou?"

"That's pretty clear," the Chief Inspector said. "You see, Miss Hamilton knew that Mrs Murray had no idea of who she was or what she looked like. It was safer in the circumstances to send another person so that should Mrs Murray take any action to report the matter to the police, the real Miss Hamilton could deny, as she has done up to now, having any knowledge of the matter. Besides, Miss Polycarpou was due to leave for Malta in a few weeks, and there wouldn't have been any trace of her in any case."

"Well," I said, "I'm glad. That more or less puts the lid on the case, doesn't it? I suppose you'll have enough now to file action against Miss Hamilton for Mr Murray's murder, wouldn't you? Seems there's a pretty strong circumstantial case."

"It appears to be reasonably conclusive, but there are one or two things that need tidying up. However, we have already filed plaint, and her case should come up shortly for hearing at the Old Bailey. We will, of course, have to get the formal sanction of the director of public prosecutions."

"That's good news," I said. "I will see you tomorrow at eleven. Bye-bye."

I couldn't help emitting a sigh of relief. Until now the mystery surrounding Don's death and the enquiries following it had kept its memory unpleasantly alive in our minds, and it was distressing that his life was being raked up before our eyes, even though he had been dead over five weeks now. There would, of course, be the bother of Miss Hamilton's trial and the attendant publicity, which would naturally be a great strain for Celia, but at least that could not go on forever. Eventually everything would be over and done with once and for all. Celia and I had to see it through before we could even think of getting married. We were still bound up with all that had happened to Don, and until the mystery of his death had been cleared, we could not feel free and at peace.

At noon I drove over to Celia's. As I entered the long drive I saw her pottering about in the garden, bending over some plants. She straightened up on hearing the engine and, flinging away her spade, came up to the porch, smiling eagerly at seeing me. I took her in my arms and kissed her.

Her face was a little moist from the work in the garden, and she smelt of earth and foliage.

"I've got some news," I said. "Chief Inspector Smith rang me up. They've found the woman who visited you – Miss Hamilton's imposter."

Celia was silent for a moment, as if her gladness at seeing me was soured by the mention of this news, which brought back the unpleasant recollection of Don's death.

Then she said quickly, "But who is she? What has she to do with all this?"

I explained Miss Polycarpou's role in the bizarre story. "Don't you see?" I said optimistically. "This fairly winds up the case. The evidence against Miss Hamilton is quite overwhelming."

"Yes," Celia said, smiling. "It is a great relief, isn't it? I do hope the case will be over soon."

We went into the house, sat on the settee in the sitting room. I held Celia around the waist, and she leaned her head on my shoulder.

Celia said, "What will they do to her if they find her guilty?"

I looked at her quizzically. There had been a note of sadness, even of concern in her question, as if she were sorry for Miss Hamilton.

"It depends," I said, "on whether her defence can bring in any extenuating circumstances that might mitigate her offence. If, however, the prosecution can prove the murder was premeditated, then it will be the death penalty for her. Otherwise, she might get away with imprisonment."

Celia sighed. Presently she said, "But supposing it can be shown that she killed him because, driven by love for him, she could not bear the torment of his neglect. Should that help to reduce her sentence?"

"Actually," I said, "there aren't any hard-and-fast rules in such matters. Such a circumstance as you mention, a crime of passion, could be considered mitigating, I suppose, but it would certainly not apply if the murder could be proved to be premeditated."

After a long pause, I said, "The Chief Inspector wants us to come over to the Yard tomorrow to identify the woman. He doesn't think it absolutely essential that you come, but you could if you wished to."

"No, I'd rather not," Celia said. "Going back to London would be too disrupting now that I've begun to settle in here. I hope you don't mind, Ben."

"Of course not," I said. "I rather thought it would be better if you didn't."

When I was ushered into Chief Inspector Smith's office the next day, Miss Polycarpou was already seated there together with a woman constable. Miss Polycarpou raised her head and looked at me with timid, frightened eyes that held the faintest ghost of recognition in them.

"Yes," I said nodding to the Chief Inspector's unspoken query. "This is the lady who called herself Miss Hamilton."

Her confession already given, she had been brought before the Chief Inspector merely for my visit. Miss Polycarpou sat with her hands in her lap, and she once again fixed her large, lambent eyes on the floor. The Inspector spoke a few words to her, to which she answered very primly and diffidently. I didn't wish to say anything to her, and when the Chief Inspector told her she could leave, I was relieved. After she had left, the Chief Inspector turned to me, and a smile brightened his face.

"I've got something else to show you," he said as he rang a bell on the desk. An elderly police sergeant entered a while later and clicked his heels.

"Anything, sir?" he queried.

"Yes, Pearson. Will you get me the file on Mrs Blaine?" This he said so casually that for a moment it did not register. Then when my mind had grasped it, I turned in surprise with an exclamation poised on my lips and saw the Chief Inspector's eyes light up with a mischievous glint.

"Mrs Blaine?" I said incredulously.

"Yes, Mrs Blaine," the Chief Inspector said. "I am afraid I forgot to tell you about it over the telephone, but we know now who she is."

"So you have traced her?" I said.

The Chief Inspector took a deep puff of his cigarette and let the smoke out through his nostrils. "No, I'm afraid not. But thanks to Mrs Bleakely, we are certain of her identity, and that makes things much easier. Although, mind you, with Mrs Blaine's criminal record, as you will see, the case against Miss Hamilton will not hold as much weight as it otherwise would have, until, that is, we can clear all suspicion from Mrs Blaine."

"But how did Mrs Bleakely help?" I asked.

"Well, at first we didn't put too much store by Mrs Blaine's disappearance, although, of course, we tried to trace her whereabouts. But these enquiries didn't yield any results in spite of the requests we published in the newspapers calling for Mrs Blaine to report to us for information about the murder. So we had reason to suspect that she may not have wanted to reveal herself. From everyone's description of her she seemed to be rather a shady character, so we were suspicious that she might have a connection with Mr Murray's death, and we thought we'd try our luck and see if our files could help us. Accordingly, we invited Mrs Bleakely to have a look at our rogues' gallery. I must say the old dear was awfully cooperative, though very sceptical. She spent practically all morning looking through our photographs, but when she came upon Mrs Blaine's, she got quite excited."

The Chief Inspector smiled. "When we showed her Mrs Blaine's file, she was so upset to think that she should have had anything to do with the police, let alone the long list of crimes given in her file."

I was eager to hear what crimes Mrs Blaine had perpetrated, but Sergeant Pearson came in with the file, so I could find out for myself.

The Chief Inspector took the folder, turned a few pages, and handed it to me. "There you have a summary of her offences and sentences."

I read through the list. There were five convictions: two for procuring, one for drug peddling, another for shoplifting, and finally one for blackmail. Her sentences ranged from fines to a total period of ten months imprisonment.

"Rather an impressive record, I must say. And quite an assortment of crimes," I said.

"Yes," the Chief Inspector said. "The usual combination of underworld crime associated with the ageing prostitute. They are all interwoven. The young woman prostitutes, then, when she no longer has her youth, she procures. Drug peddling and theft are an easy way out during bad periods; and, of course, rich clients, particularly married ones and those high up on the social register, provide easy prey for blackmail."

I idly turned back the pages of the dossier. What I came upon made my blood freeze. I must have uttered an exclamation or gone pale or both, for I suddenly heard the Chief Inspector's voice as if from far away saying, "Mr Benison, is there anything the matter? Are you all right?"

"Yes, yes," I said. "I am all right. I wasn't feeling too well all of a sudden."

I looked again at the photograph of Mrs Blaine on the first page of the dossier and knew that there could be no doubt about it. I was not mistaken. It was an impressive face not for its beauty or character but for its ugliness and depravity. It was a face that expressed more clearly than words the degeneracy of her life. The hair hung loosely on either side of her face in thin wisps, accentuating the narrow, weasel eyes with the puffed eyelids and the thick, arched, caterpillar eyebrows. Her broad, corrugated forehead, large aquiline nose with flared nostrils, and the severely chapped mouth completed the picture.

"Do you recognise her?" the Chief Inspector asked, and I had to lie to him. I don't know why I lied, but I felt instinctively that my doing so would in some way be in Celia's interest, for the woman I had seen talking to Celia at the Marble Arch Tube station a few days back was none other than Mrs Blaine! I had to keep this knowledge a secret until I had first had a chance to talk to Celia.

"No, no, Chief Inspector," I said. "The face seemed familiar, but I was mistaken."

The Chief Inspector looked at me quizzically, and then his brow relaxed. "Isn't it amazing how many people one meets who remind us of others we have known?" There was no inflection in his voice to suggest anything other than that he had accepted my explanation. I was sure that he believed me.

The Chief Inspector invited me to lunch, but my mind was too engaged in trying to sort out the mystery of what had happened, and I had an irrepressible urge to get to Wimbledon with all speed and ask Celia what it all meant. I declined his offer, saying that I had some important matters to attend to, and took my leave. As he followed me to the door, the Chief Inspector enquired about Celia and requested I convey his regards to her.

I reproached myself for having left the Chief Inspector's company so abruptly, but my mind was in a torment trying to sort out some sense from what had transpired. It seemed ridiculous that Celia and Mrs Blaine should have anything to do with each other, but not even by the furthest stretch of my imagination could I find an answer to the situation.

Chapter 15

I took a taxi to the station. I had a few minutes to wait for the train, so I bought myself a cup of tea at the station's restaurant. An ugly thought kept rising in my mind, but I chided myself for having so much as entertained it. I gulped my tea and walked up and down the platform restlessly until the train arrived.

The first-class compartment was empty except for an old grey-haired gentleman and an equally old lady who was probably his wife. I sat down in a corner engrossed in my thoughts. Suddenly from some deep recess in my subconscious flitted a recollection through my mind. The matter had completely slipped my mind, although at the time it happened it had made an impression on me. Now under the pressure it had surfaced. I remembered that on that day in London whilst looking out of my window and seeing Celia coming up the street, I had seen a man who had been walking some distance behind her try to conceal his face from me. It did cross my mind at the time that the man had not wished to be seen and that he had been following her. I also recalled his deliberately pulling his cap over his face on passing under my window. But the joy and surprise of seeing Celia after such a long absence had blotted this out, and I hadn't given it any further thought.

Now, however, it kept intruding upon my mind and adding a sense of mystery. It could, of course, mean nothing – I knew that there could be all sorts of simple explanations for such an incident – but it still bothered me.

Quite suddenly again, my mind turned a corner and yet another incident – trivial, for all intents and purposes – now loomed. It was that mysterious telephone call for Celia late in the night a few days back, from a woman. Perhaps it had been Mrs Blaine?

It was with apprehension that, having got off at Wimbledon, I took a taxi to Celia's residence. I was eager to hear from her concerning Mrs Blaine, but I felt a peculiar sense of anxiety, an odd impatience in the taxi, and I was greatly relieved when it came within view of the house. Presently it came to a halt under the porch, and I got out. An absolute stillness pervaded the house and its grounds. It was a sultry day and the sun's rays shone brightly and warmed my back as I stood at the door and rang the bell. I waited for a while but no one answered, so I rang again, giving it a long press before leaving off. After a further wait, I was about to ring once more when I heard a shuffling of feet inside and the door opened, revealing not Celia but Mrs Feston. I asked her where Celia was, and Mrs Feston informed me that she had gone out to make some purchases but should be back any time now. It was stuffy inside and little beads of perspiration prickled my skin and collected under my shirt. I removed my jacket and draped it over a chair. Mrs Feston apologised for the delay in opening the door, saying she had been upstairs. She seated herself on one of the settees and took up some knitting she had brought with her, and I eased myself into the comfort of one of Celia's deep, velvet chairs.

"You seem upset," said Mrs Feston, peeping kindly over her horn-rimmed spectacles.

"I'm tired," I said and tried to smile.

"It's none of my business," Mrs Feston said after a while, "but you two should get married. It will do Celia a world of good. She worries so, poor thing."

"Does she worry much?" I asked. "I thought she had settled down to being her normal self. She seems quite cheerful."

"I'm not at all sure about that. She seems all right when you're about, but when you're away she gets to brooding and is quite restless. You should have seen her this morning before she went out. She seemed terribly upset, almost scared, and had a faraway look in her eyes – it frightened me, it really did. Something must have upset her. Mr Benison, please speak to her – she needs you. Her nerves have gone to pieces since Mr Murray's death. It's only natural, poor child."

"I didn't know that she worried so," I said with genuine concern. "Do you know what seems to be troubling her?"

It pained me to know that Celia was in anguish. I had grown to love her so much that my soul was sensitive to her every whim and emotion, and to hear of her secret unhappiness wrung my heartstrings and evoked within me tender sympathy.

Mrs Feston evidently felt the same way. She always had Celia's interest at heart, and I understood only too well her concern for Celia's happiness.

In answer to my question of the source of Celia's trouble, she put aside her knitting and wrinkled her brows as if she were trying to fathom out some mystery. She said, "I don't really know, but I've never seen her like this before. She seems all right when she's with me, but then she's always managed to conceal her feelings well. She's always been a deep one, you know. Hates making a show of her feelings and has since childhood, but she can't stand much. I don't suppose I would have guessed but for what I chanced to see this morning."

Mrs Feston's face clouded, and she leaned forward confidentially. I waited apprehensively to hear what she had to say.

"I had just put the breakfast things away and sat down on this very chair to read the morning newspapers when I heard Celia's voice upstairs as if she were speaking to someone. I had taken her breakfast to her in bed, as she had complained of not feeling too well, and I knew, of course, that she was alone. So naturally I was surprised that I should hear her voice as if in conversation. I waited awhile and didn't hear anything more, so I presumed that I had been mistaken. But a little later I heard her speak again, and I thought I detected the sound of stifled sobs."

Mrs Feston pushed her drooping spectacles up the bridge of her nose and, clasping her wrinkled hands nervously in front of her, continued her tale. "I feared that Celia was in pain, so I called out her name. But hearing no reply, I went up to investigate. I knew that it was more than likely that she hadn't heard me, as her room is at the end of the corridor, along the west wing of the house, as you know. I climbed up the stairs without waiting for an answer, and as I reached the top, I heard Celia utter what seemed like an imprecation. I didn't want to snoop, and I couldn't help feeling that I must not disturb Celia, but I tiptoed along the corridor to her room. The door was ajar, and I saw her seated on the side of the bed, her body hunched over her knees, shaking with sobs. She didn't see me and I didn't want to embarrass her by bursting in at such a time. I was about to leave when I distinctly heard her cry, 'Oh, why won't she leave me in peace!' and then, 'I must do it. There is no other way.'"

Mrs Feston leaned forward and blinked nervously. "Now what do you suppose she meant, Mr Benison?"

I was equally at a loss to interpret what Celia could have meant, but my mind was already building up all kinds of connections. Foremost was the thought that Celia's remark must have applied to Mrs Blaine, but I couldn't see what the context might be. I hovered over first one theory then another, but none of them seemed to make sense.

"I don't know," I said, perplexed. "I really couldn't say, Mrs Feston. Was there a sequel to all this? What happened afterwards? Did you leave?"

"Yes. I didn't want to be seen. I felt almost guilty. You understand, don't you? So I tiptoed back downstairs and came right back here. It wasn't long before Celia came down herself. She had made an effort to do herself up a bit, but her eyes were still bloodshot, and although she affected a cheerful manner, she looked weary and forlorn. She spent the whole morning pottering around in the garden. After we had lunch she said she had to go into town for some provisions, and that's where she is now."

I fetched my pipe from my coat pocket, filled it with tobacco from my pouch, and lit it. I needed to calm the vague agitation in my breast. Mrs Feston's news of Celia's conduct, which spoke so plainly of her unhappiness, greatly grieved me. But it wasn't just that. I kept trying to fathom what was behind Celia's unhappiness. What could she have meant by those vengeful words? To whom had she referred? Was it to Mrs Blaine, and if so, why? What power could Mrs Blaine have over her? Or could it be that she was referring to some other mysterious person? And again, what had she meant?

I wondered if Celia's words could have been merely the ramblings of an overwrought mind and bore no relevance to actuality. Such a supposition seemed to make sense, except that I had seen Celia with Mrs Blaine, and that could not be rationalised away.

"Mr Benison." Mrs Feston's voice cut into my thoughts. Her tone was tentative, and I responded instinctively to it.

"What is it, Mrs Feston?"

She seemed perturbed. "I really don't know if I should tell you, Mr Benison. It's about Celia's car. I promised Celia that I wouldn't. She made me promise not to mention it to anyone, but I am sure it would be all right to tell you. I feel awful about it, though. Do you think she'll mind?"

I was about to reply that it was entirely up to her when the doorbell rang. Mrs Feston gave a nervous gasp and looked terribly flustered, poor thing. It had all been too much for her. I walked over and opened the door.

It was Celia.

It occurred to me with a feeling of sudden discomfort that if Celia had been standing by the door for even a little while before ringing the bell, she may have heard our conversation. Mrs Feston's voice was normally clear and sharp, and the door, with its wide grille above it, was only a few feet away from where Mrs Feston sat. It wasn't unusual that we wouldn't have heard Celia, as her footsteps would have been muffled on the well-trimmed front lawn. The garage was a little way off, and from inside the house, one could hardly hear the car being driven in. I may have been imagining, of course, but I thought that for a moment Celia's eyes gave an expression that indicated she had overheard something of our conversation. But I couldn't be sure, and it was more than likely just my imagination.

Celia was carrying a basket of parcels, and she greeted me happily. Mrs Feston was still looking at sixes and sevens. She relieved Celia of the basket and took it into the pantry.

"Did you have a busy day?" I asked.

"One gets so worn out in this heat," Celia said, wiping the perspiration from her brow and stuffing the handkerchief into her pocket. "I'm glad you're back," she continued, smiling at me. "I've great news, and I've wanted to tell you but haven't had the chance."

I was distracted by my own thoughts and must have appeared so, for she reproached me with, "Aren't you interested in what I've got to say? I think you'll be most interested."

"Oh," I said from far away. "What is it?"

"I have met Mrs Blaine."

At first I felt a startled relief. It had so worried me why Celia should have had anything to do with Mrs Blaine, and I had been particularly concerned about why she hadn't told me of it, that now her having done so seemed to put everything above suspicion. At last the mystery was to be unravelled, and I was eager to hear what she had to say.

"I know," I said. "I saw you talk to her at the Tube station. But why didn't you tell me sooner? I've been so worried."

A shadow crossed her face for an instant, but she said, "Oh, so it was no surprise. What a shame, I thought I'd surprise you and you've known all the time. But how did you know it was Mrs Blaine?"

I decided to sit down. "But why did Mrs Blaine contact you? What was her purpose in doing so?" I said, ignoring her question.

"Well, she said she was so shaken up when she heard the police had been looking for her that she panicked. Not knowing where to turn, she thought she'd contact me for advice, as she had important evidence which she felt she should confide to me. So she tried to ring me here, but Mrs Feston informed her that I'd gone to the Havershams' and gave her their telephone number, and then she contacted me."

I was silent for a moment, trying to process this information. "But why didn't you tell me all this while?" I asked, genuinely perplexed.

Celia sat up in her chair, her hands clasped in front of her. "I would have, Ben, except that Mrs Blaine requested that I not tell a soul because she had made up her mind to go to the police herself and didn't want them to come looking for her. You see, she said she had heard of Don's death only by accident, when reading a recent edition of the *Times* and seeing that the police were still looking for her for questioning in connection with the murder. She was afraid that if her whereabouts had been leaked to the police before she went to them, they might think she was trying to evade arrest. So you see, I didn't want to mention it to you because you were going to see Chief Inspector Smith and it would have been embarrassing for you if he had brought up the subject of Mrs Blaine."

"But, Celia," I said, "the woman hasn't given herself up. How do you know she will?"

"Of course she will," Celia said. "Why shouldn't she? She has no reason to fear the police. She says she saw Miss Hamilton come out of Don's room the evening he was killed."

"But how could she know who Miss Hamilton is?"

"She doesn't know Miss Hamilton, but she says the description printed in the newspaper seems to fit the woman she saw. She mentioned the leopard-skin cape. Besides, she says she can quite easily identify her."

"Unfortunately, Mrs Blaine's evidence won't be of any value, really. Miss Hamilton has herself admitted to visiting Don's room, and the taxi driver's statement confirms it."

"Well, not really," said Celia. "Mrs Blaine's evidence amounts to more than just that. She says she saw Miss Hamilton leave Don's room not once but twice that night. And that might explain how the gas tap came to be closed."

"Twice?" I said, baffled. I was eager to hear what connection this could have to the gas tap being closed.

"Yes, Ben," Celia said. "Mrs Blaine is positive of that. She says the door of her room, which was next to Don's, was ajar, and she was knitting when she heard footsteps along the corridor and someone knocking on Don's door. She stepped out of her room, out of curiosity, in time to see Don open the door, say something, and let the woman in. She says she had a brief glimpse of the woman's profile and noticed the leopard-skin cape. About half an hour or so later, she says she heard Don's door open again, and she quickly stepped out of her room just in time to see the woman with the leopard-skin cape leave the building. Mrs

Blaine says she was about to return to her room when she heard the front door squeak open slowly, and she could see the image of the woman in the leopard skin cape – who must have decided to return – through the glass on the door. She hastily hid in the shadows under the staircase. The woman seemed agitated and took a key from over Don's door and opened it, which struck Mrs Blaine as odd – it was as if Don was not in his room. She says she noticed that the woman's left hand was gloved but the right, which held the key, was ungloved. The woman entered Don's room and was back in a trice holding a glove to her nose and coughing faintly. It occurred to Mrs Blaine then that the woman had returned to retrieve her glove, which she must have forgotten when she went out the first time. I'm sure," Celia concluded, "that, without thinking, Miss Hamilton must have closed the gas tap when she went back in because it must have been suffocating and Don was already dead. Incidentally, Mrs Blaine says that while she was hiding under the staircase, she saw Miss Proust ascend the staircase, which squares with Miss Proust's account of having visited Mrs Blaine's room at around the same time but having found her to be out."

"How did Mrs Blaine explain her sudden departure?"

Celia said that she had asked her precisely that question but was satisfied with her answer, as to prove it, she had a telegram which she said the postman had brought the same night, about half an hour after she had returned to her room. It was from a friend in Sussex who boarded Mrs Blaine's ten-year-old nephew attending school there, saying the boy had been knocked down by a car and was in hospital. Mrs Blaine had taken over the care of the boy when her widowed sister had died some years back and was devoted to him. She said she had been terribly overcome by this news and had decided to leave at once. She had already paid her rent for the week but went down to inform Mrs Bleakely of her absence, but not finding her in, had left her a message, packed her things, and left. Thereafter, she had been terribly anxious while visiting her nephew in hospital and hadn't the time or inclination to contact Mrs Bleakely again.

"Well, that puts the lid on Miss Hamilton," I said, relieved that the mysterious events had been so satisfactorily resolved. It could be easily surmised, as Celia had pointed out, that it was she who closed the gas tap. One thought, however, came to mind.

"Was Mrs Blaine our mysterious caller a few nights back?" I asked.

"Yes," Celia said casually. "She was trying to get in touch with me but was put out when she heard your voice and rang off. She called me the next day and said that she had been delayed in going to the police since our meeting, as she had been taken ill with a severe migraine, but that she was going to do so right away."

I could see that Celia's long account of Mrs Blaine's story had wearied her, leaving her a trifle pale and overwrought.

"Don't be unhappy, dear," I said, putting my hand on hers. "It won't be long now, and then we can forget all about it. You really mustn't worry so much. Mrs Feston said you were terribly upset this morning. I think you need a holiday once this whole business is over and done with."

"I know, darling," Celia said. "I must be such a terrible bother to you. I promise to cheer up. You do love me, don't you?"

"Very much."

"Always?"

"Always and ever."

True to her word, Mrs Blaine reported to the police, and the Chief Inspector called me in my office to apprise me of this fact. At Celia's request, I did not divulge to him that Mrs Blaine had contacted her and that I was aware of Mrs Blaine's promise to report to the police. Celia said she did not see any point in telling the police of her meeting with Mrs Blaine, as it would have no material bearing on the case and would only result in her being dragged into the proceedings. The Chief Inspector also informed me that the public prosecutor had agreed to bring the case to trial.

Chapter 16

The trial of Ada Hamilton began on a bleak autumn day at the Old Bailey. The newspapers had given much publicity to it, referring to Miss Hamilton as the "Maltese Murderess", the "Mysterious Maltese", the "Lovely Murderess from Malta", and a score of other similar epithets. The case aroused public interest, not so much out of horror as human curiosity, roused mainly by the personal charms of Miss Hamilton, whose photograph had appeared in every newspaper in the country. A large number of people were moved by pity, not for Don Murray but for Celia, who had had to endure not only her husband's infidelity but also his death under such terrible circumstances. The newspapers encouraged and in a way instigated this sympathy, portraying Celia as the wronged wife, who, despite her husband's affairs, had loved him and had tried hard to keep her marriage secure.

I had left Wimbledon early to be on time for the first day's proceedings at the Old Bailey. Celia had expressed her disinclination to attend the trial from the very start and stayed back at Craven Manor. It was only natural that the ordeal of the trial, which would uncover the gruesome details of Don's death and his relationship with Miss Hamilton, would be distasteful to her. I had planned to stay in London so that it would be convenient to attend the trial but decided instead to travel daily from Wimbledon until such time as it was expedient for Celia to also come to London.

The first day of the trial began with the bustle that is the hallmark of all first days. The people who had come to watch the trial weren't yet used to their surroundings, and the police were extra busy controlling the crowds and showing people their seats. The newspapermen hustled each other in the corridors, their cameras in hand to get those first vital shots which would give the scoop to their respective papers. Even those eminent gentlemen who were to be the chief protagonists in the forthcoming drama – the prosecutor and the counsel for the defence – and those twelve good and true men and women of the jury were all in a state of restrained agitation, excited by the novelty of the day.

Presently, however, quietness descended upon the court as the accused was brought into the box, and all eyes instinctively turned to her. She wore a plain grey cotton dress with red buttons down the front. It was at once refreshingly simple and elegant, emphasising the well-rounded proportions of her body. Her hair was tied in a bun, bringing into relief the delicate lines of her face.

After the initial formalities, the case began. Mr Emanuel Pritt, QC, rose from his seat, coughed into his handkerchief and, settling his gown on his shoulders, began his opening speech for the Crown. "May it please My Lord and members of the jury, in this my opening address, I shall put before you the facts on which the prosecution's case rests. In order to do this, it is necessary that I give you some idea of the defendant's background and her relationship with the deceased, Don Murray."

In clear, precise language, he outlined Miss Hamilton's history from the time of her arrival in England. "Like many of her countrymen, she came to England five years ago seeking better prospects for the future. Unlike many of them, she was not satisfied with the stability and standard of life that a steady job in this country offered. After working for a few months as a salesgirl in a Woolworth's store in Birmingham, she left of her own accord, and from then on earned her living, in the main, as a woman of the streets. After two years of such a life, she moved from Birmingham to London, where she put up at lodgings in Notting Hill Gate and continued to carry on the life of a prostitute."

Mr Pritt paused, looked at the jury, and adjusted his horn-rimmed spectacles. He went on to recount how Don Murray and Ada Hamilton had met and the circumstances leading to the break in their relationship. He said that the defendant had been considerably upset by this breach in her relationship with the deceased and had appeared to have tried on numerous occasions to revive their association, but without success.

"Her desire to do so," he said, "is evident from the fact that she even went so far as to tell him that she was pregnant and that he was responsible, although, in actual fact, she had not conceived. As mentioned, Miss Hamilton was greatly disturbed by the break in her relations with Mr Murray, the deceased, for whom she had more than an ordinary attachment. There could not be any other reason for Miss Hamilton's persistence – and certainly not any mercenary motive, for the deceased was not a wealthy man."

He paused for effect, looked at the jury, and continued.

"We next come to a fresh aspect of the case – an aspect that, though isolated in itself, will be shown to have a connection to the crime and will provide an insight into Miss Hamilton's mentality and her motives.

"Miss Hamilton has a cousin, a Miss Charlotte Polycarpou of London, a young woman who has for some time now been employed as a trainee nurse at St Mary's Hospital in Paddington. Although they are first cousins, their relationship was only a perfunctory one, and Miss Hamilton managed to conceal from her cousin her way of life. In fact, Miss Polycarpou had always been given to understand that Miss Hamilton was employed as a clerk in a West End firm, earning a salary of £20 a week. Miss Hamilton had told Miss Polycarpou so on one occasion when Miss Polycarpou had approached her for a loan of

£150, which she had wanted to send to her parents in Malta who were in poor circumstances and in poorer health. Miss Hamilton had given her £50 and said that was all she could afford. The cousins had thereafter met on one or two occasions for short spells. Sometime in April of this year, Miss Polycarpou had received an urgent letter from her father stating that her mother was seriously ill and that the doctors had diagnosed the ailment as a tumour of the brain and that the only chance of saving her life was an immediate operation which would cost approximately £5,000. Miss Polycarpou had been terribly upset by this news and had gone to see Miss Hamilton for advice and assistance. Miss Hamilton had told her that she could not afford anything like that sum but had outlined a scheme whereby she could obtain it. Her scheme was a diabolical one aimed at exposing Mr Murray and breaking up his marriage. She instigated Miss Polycarpou to go to Mrs Murray, who was in Wimbledon, and blackmail her into paying the required sum. Miss Polycarpou had protested but, in her desperation, had finally agreed. Armed with some letters which Miss Hamilton had given her as evidence of her association with Mr Murray, Miss Polycarpou visited Mrs Murray and, calling herself Miss Hamilton, showed Mrs Murray the letters, threatening, as her cousin had told her to, that she was carrying Mr Murray's child that she needed money to have an abortion. Mrs Murray had sought the assistance of a friend, Mr Benison, who is a solicitor, and he advised that no payment be made until Mr Murray was consulted. Mr Benison told Miss Polycarpou that he would have to see Mr Murray first and set off to London that very day for this purpose. There he met Mr Murray, who expressed his wish to first see Miss Hamilton and come to some terms with her. Mr Benison thereafter returned to Wimbledon."

The Prosecutor then went on to give a statement of Miss Hamilton's guilt. In brief, simple sentences, he outlined the evidence against her, starting with the mendacity of her own statement to the police and the attempts to conceal information of her movements on the evening in question and winding up with the telling eyewitness evidence of Mrs Blaine's.

By the time he had finished, the evidence against Miss Ada Hamilton looked overwhelming, and it seemed as if the defence would need a miracle to save her.

After the opening address, the Prosecutor called his first witness, Sergeant Barnes of the Oxford Street Police. He was a thickset man in his mid-forties. He sported a scorpion of a moustache and gave his testimony with the assurance of a man to whom giving evidence in court was more or less routine. He had a thick cockney accent and, from time to time, wiped his moustache with the back of his hand while he spoke. He gave an account of his visit to the deceased's room. He recounted that he had received a call from Mrs Bleakely, the landlady, at approximately ten thirty p.m. on 16 July to the effect that one of her tenants had been found gassed in his room and appeared to be dead. He had immediately proceeded with Constable Ruperts to the scene of the incident.

"When I entered the deceased's room, there was a strong smell of gas. I noticed that the windows were closed, and I instructed constable Ruperts to open them, which 'e did. My next step was to close the gas tap, but on examining it, I found it to be already tightly secured. I brought this to the notice of Constable Ruperts at the time. I next examined the deceased, who was lying under the sheets in 'is bed, and 'e appeared to 'ave been dead for some time. Rigor mortis 'ad already set in. I also noticed a glass on the dressing table close to the bed. On examination, I found that it smelled strongly of whisky.

"I next questioned the maid, Miss Caverill, who stated that she'd been passing by Mr Murray's door on 'er way out to 'ave some coffee at the coffee shop down the road when she was assailed with the smell of gas from Mr Murray's room. She immediately informed Mrs Bleakely, the landlady, about it. I next questioned Mrs Bleakely, who stated that she was in 'er room in the basement when Miss Caverill came down and informed 'er that there appeared to be a strong smell of gas from Mr Murray's room. She immediately went upstairs to Mr Murray's room and thereafter rang up the police."

After the Sergeant had finished giving his testimony, Mr Pritt questioned him. "Sergeant Barnes, were you certain that the gas tap was closed when you checked it?"

"Very definitely, sir."

"Didn't this surprise you?"

"I'd say it did, sir. But at first I thought the maid or Mrs Bleakely may 'ave closed it."

"Did you make enquiries as to how the tap came to be closed?"

"Very definitely, sir. I asked Miss Caverill and Mrs Bleakely if they'd closed it, and they said they'd barely gone into the room."

"Were any of the windows in the deceased's room open when you went in?"

"As I've already mentioned, they were closed, sir. I 'ad to ask Constable Ruperts to open them."

"So no attempt had been made by anyone to even open the windows?"

"Very definitely not, sir."

"One more question, Sergeant. Can you briefly, in your own words, describe to us how you found the deceased when you first entered the room?"

"I found the deceased lying on 'is left side in bed with 'is face towards the gas heater. Only 'is face was visible, as the rest of 'is body was under the bedclothes."

"From what you saw at the time, was there anything to indicate a struggle or any kind of disorder? Would you say, from your observation of the deceased and the condition of his bed and so on that there were any signs of violence or disarray?"

"No, I cannot think of any indications of disarray or violence, sir. Everything in the room was tidy and in perfect order. The deceased 'imself was lying neatly and comfortably tucked up in 'is bed. No, I'd say there was nothing to suggest disorder or violence of any sort, sir."

"Thank you, Sergeant. That will be all."

The counsel for the defence, Sir Charles Quipper, rose to his feet. "Tell me, Sergeant, were there any fingerprints on the glass?"

"Yes."

"Whose were they?"

"Mr Murray's."

"Isn't it also a fact that a half-consumed bottle of whisky was also found and examined for fingerprints?"

"Yes, sir. That is correct."

"And can you tell us whose fingerprints were found on it?"

"Mr Murray's."

"Were there any other prints?"

"No."

"Thank you, Sergeant."

The next witness to be called was myself. I was formally dressed in a black pinstriped suit, plain white shirt, and black-and-white striped tie. As I walked to the witness box, people's heads turned in my direction. A smartly dressed policeman stood erect at the entrance to the court. A woman's discreet cough broke the silence as I took the stand and was sworn in.

After having elicited the details of my visit to see Don, Mr Pritt went on to question me.

"Mr Benison, you are quite certain that you did not tell the deceased that his wife knew of Miss Hamilton's visit?"

"Yes. It was Mrs Murray's wish that I keep this from him. She wanted to be the one to tell him. That is why I told him that the woman had come to my place and not, as it happened, to Mrs Murray's."

"So the deceased was still hopeful that he could come to some kind of arrangement with the accused before news got through to his wife? I take it, of course, that the deceased was particularly concerned that his wife should not hear about his misconduct with the accused?"

"Oh yes. It was of great importance to him that his wife should not know about it, and he expressed great relief when I told him that she did not know."

I could see what he was getting at: Mr Pritt was trying to take the wind out of the defence's likely plea that Don had committed suicide in a fit of depression and that Adriana Hamilton had merely stumbled upon his dead body.

Sir Charles's questions in cross-examination proved how correct this assumption was.

"Mr Benison, you did tell Mr Murray that the woman whom you had met had asked for a large sum of money, a sum which he could ill afford?"

"Yes."

"You also mentioned to him that she had threatened to expose him to the Church authorities, did you not?"

"I did."

"That would have most probably meant dismissal for Mr Murray given his position, wouldn't it?"

"Yes, it would."

"Did Mr Murray know this?"

"Yes."

"Mr Benison, was the deceased fond of his wife? Would you say he was deeply in love with her?"

"Yes, he was very devoted to her."

"And the deceased, although he had lived a loose life before his marriage, had, to the best of your knowledge, but for this unfortunate incident, turned over a new leaf?"

"Yes."

"And from your knowledge of him, would you say that this change was primarily due to his love for his wife and the fact that he did not want to risk offending her?"

"Yes, I suppose so."

Sir Charles paused, walked towards the box, and spoke in a firm, assertive voice. "Would you say that Mrs Murray was not the sort of person who could accept or condone unfaithfulness on the part of her husband?"

"I think she would find it very difficult to condone such conduct."

"And the deceased knew that if his wife found out about him, it could well mean the end of his marriage?"

"Yes, I suppose so."

"So if his relations with Miss Hamilton came to light, Mr Murray would have had to face not only possible dismissal and disgrace, but also the ruin of his marriage?"

"Yes, I suppose it would have meant all that."

"That will be all, Mr Benison. Thank you."

I was about to leave the box when Mr Pritt decided to re-examine me. He stood up and walked slowly across the courtroom and spoke in a low, clear voice. "Mr Benison, for how long did you know the deceased?"

"For the better part of fifteen years."

"Did you know him intimately?"

"Yes, we were very close friends."

"From your knowledge of him, Mr Benison, would you say that he was a man who was easily given to depression?"

Before I could answer, Sir Charles Quipper rose from his seat. "My Lord, I object to Learned Counsel seeking an opinion. The facts must indicate whether—"

"Objection overruled," Judge Brecket's voice came down firmly. "The question is pertinent."

Sir Charles shrugged and sat down; Judge Brecket had a reputation for sticking to his decisions, and it wouldn't do any good to offend him. Mr Pritt repeated his question to me.

"No," I said. "He was rarely bowled over by anything. Nothing could really worry him, much. He took life as it came."

"Thank you, Mr Benison. That will be all."

The prosecution next called Dr Strompet, the pathologist. He was a small, sprucely dressed man of solemn countenance. His voice carried authority and commanded respect. He stated briefly that the autopsy had revealed death due to respiratory failure caused by carbon monoxide poisoning. A certain quantity of barbiturate, a strong soporific, was also found, although not in large enough quantities to cause death. An examination of the contents of the glass found in the deceased's room showed traces of the same drug mixed in alcohol – the drug had been taken with the whisky.

Mr Pritt paced slowly and deliberately in front of the witness box. Presently he faced the doctor and said, "Dr Strompet, the deceased was found dead of carbon monoxide poisoning neatly and comfortably tucked under the blankets in his bed with the gas tap closed." He paused. "Now, if we were to assume for argument's sake that the deceased took his own life, however unlikely this may seem, would it have been possible for him, after having taken the sleeping draught, to have opened the gas tap, inhaled a sufficiently lethal quantity of gas, and thereafter closed the tap and repaired to bed, there to wait until death overtook him?"

Dr Strompet could hardly restrain a smile at the tone of Mr Pritt's interrogation.

"Most unlikely, indeed," he said.

"And can you tell the Court why, Doctor?"

"Well, yes. It is not possible to inhale a lethal quantity of gas and store it away in one's lungs over a prolonged period. If such a quantity had been inhaled, the effect would have been more or less immediate. It certainly would not have given the deceased time to have walked to his bed and to have adjusted himself comfortably under his blankets."

"Thank you, Doctor. That will be all," Mr Pritt said and sat down.

Sir Charles Quipper rose slowly to his feet and, resting his hands on the desk in front of him, faced the doctor. "Isn't it possible, Doctor, that the deceased may have inhaled a substantial quantity of gas that was not a lethal amount, and that he may have closed the tap for reasons unknown to us and then crept into his bed half-dazed and been killed thereafter by the remaining gas afloat in the room?"

"No, I am afraid not. Unless there is a steady stream of gas, the carbon monoxide loses strength when mixed with the oxygen in the air. The fact that the deceased moved into his bed, a distance of about five feet away from the gas tap, should have had the very opposite effect of helping him recover from the ill effects of the carbon monoxide he would have inhaled."

Mr Pritt rose to re-examine the witness. "In other words, Doctor, what you are, in fact, saying is that the deceased himself could not have been responsible for closing the tap – or, to put it differently, it had to be someone else who closed the tap."

Mr Pritt paused to allow the impact of the sentence to sink in. Then turning slowly towards the jury, he said in a well-modulated voice, "I put it to you that the deceased could not have taken his own life. I put it to you that someone known to the deceased, having first introduced a strong sleeping draught into his drink, helped him to his bed and thereafter opened the gas tap in the full knowledge that the deceased would be well under sedation and oblivious to what was happening. And it is our intention to show beyond any shadow of doubt that the person responsible for this diabolical murder is none other than the accused, Miss Hamilton."

The next witness to be called was the taxi driver, a weedy, bespectacled little man who stood with his hands clasped in front of him, his shoulders drooping. He had a scared look on his face and an incessant nervous twitch of the neck, as if his collar was too tight and he was trying to get free of it. His testimony to the effect that he had driven Adriana Hamilton on the night of the incident to Mr Murray's hotel at around nine was elicited briefly and quickly and was mostly valuable as corroborative evidence.

The highlight of the case was the evidence of Mrs Blaine. True to form, she presented quite a grotesque spectacle and drew the attention and amusement of the crowd. She wore a gaudy pink and crimson blouse that heightened the garishness of her heavily rouged cheeks and overly painted mouth. When she spoke, her voice was hoarse. I sat enthralled as Mrs Blaine told her story.

She began by stating that at a little past nine p.m. on the day in question, she had just returned to her room from shopping when she heard voices outside in the corridor, opposite Mr Murray's room. From there she described the events exactly as Celia had told them to me: she saw the woman with the leopard-skin cape enter Mr Murray's room and then later leave, wearing just one glove. The woman returned shortly afterwards, let herself into Mr Murray's room with the key above the door, and then left again, holding her second glove, which she must have come back to collect, over her face. Mrs Blaine recognised her as the accused.

After the Prosecutor's address, the court recessed for lunch, and I decided to call Celia and apprise her of the day's proceedings before getting a bite. Celia picked up the phone and seemed to be greatly agitated.

"Oh, Ben!" she said. "Mrs Feston's had a terrible accident and the ambulance has just arrived. She tripped on the landing and rolled down the stairs and has been unconscious for the last twenty-five minutes. She's got a nasty gash on her forehead and is having a bad nosebleed. I am in a terrible lather. I must leave now, as the ambulance men have come in to remove her. Please call as soon as you arrive – must go now. Don't worry, I'll be all right."

"Awfully sorry to hear of this," I said, "but do keep calm. I'll try and come as soon as possible. Bye, darling, and be brave."

Chapter 17

When I reached Wimbledon it was already dark and a thin fog hung about the streets. I took a taxi from the station and went home. I needed a drink and a bath before going to the hospital. Poor Mrs Feston! It was a pity that she should have had such an unfortunate accident. I wondered if she had regained consciousness since her fall. I was about to ring the hospital and speak to Celia when she called me. She informed me that Mrs Feston was still delirious and had only had momentary spells of consciousness. The doctors were unable to state whether her condition would deteriorate or improve; it would largely depend on what happened in the next twenty-four hours. If her condition improved, there was every chance of a recovery. She had sustained a fracture of the front of the skull resulting in bleeding through her nose. There was hope of recovery, although her age was a factor against her. I told Celia that I would come over as soon as I could and hung up.

I took a taxi to the hospital. It was visiting time and there were the usual complement of visitors. At the end of the corridor I ran into the matron, Sister Elfreda, who was busily supervising her staff with her usual punctiliousness. We had had occasion to meet before, during a week's spell I had in hospital following a hernia operation about six months before. She was an enormous hawk-nosed woman with the most formidable countenance anyone had seen, but her eyes, which were large and soft, showed that beneath that stern exterior lurked a kind soul.

"Good evening, Mr Benison," she said, smiling brightly. "Nice to see you again. Mrs Feston is doing better. We hope she will recover. She certainly seems to show signs of improving. Mrs Murray told me you would be coming to visit her."

"I am glad to hear that," I said. "Is she still unconscious?"

"Yes, I am afraid she hasn't fully regained consciousness yet, though she has had short spells from time to time. She seems worried ... er ... afraid, Mr Benison, and has been calling out for you. But it will be a while before she may regain consciousness."

I thanked Sister Elfreda and went to meet Celia. She greeted me, and I kissed her on the forehead. She seemed very worried. Mrs Feston was lying on her side and breathing heavily when I came in. A nurse stood by her wiping the spittle from her mouth and dampening her brow with a cloth that smelt strongly of eau de cologne. I moved to the side of the bed. Mrs Feston's eyes were closed, but in an instant, they opened and sought my face. She started with recognition and an expression of relief filled her face. My presence must have comforted her. She indicated with a weary nod that I draw near to her. I was about to comply when I felt a hand on my shoulder. Turning, I beheld Celia with a finger to her lips cautioning me not to talk. She drew me gently yet firmly away.

"Strict instructions from the doctor," she whispered. "Mrs Feston must not be spoken to or speak. Her mind and body need the strictest rest. Her life depends on it."

Mrs Feston turned her head, and her eyes were wide open. She seemed to be fully conscious. Her mouth moved slowly and the words came out with an effort, but they were clear and quite audible: "Don't leave me … I am afraid … stairs." Her head flopped back onto the pillow, her eyes closed, and she breathed heavily.

Mrs Feston's appeal had left me feeling uncomfortable. It was odd that, although Celia and I were standing beside each other, she had addressed only me. Yes, there could be no doubt about it – she spoke directly to me, and something in her tone and the frightened look in her eyes held an awful urgency, an almost desperate imploring, which touched me deeply. It was some time before I could shake off its effect. Her words were uncanny, as if she were trying to tell me something terribly important, yet I had the curious feeling when I watched her that a part of her mind wanted to hold something back.

"She is half delirious," I heard Celia say. "She's been saying the most curious things. You mustn't let it puzzle you."

Celia placed her fingers so gently on my arm and smiled.

"Yes, of course," I said. "The poor thing's rather confused."

"There's nothing to worry about," Celia said. "I shall be here to attend to her. The doctor has given me permission to stay on until lights out. He says she should be better tomorrow unless her body weakens. I am sure she'll be okay."

Sister Elfreda came into the room. She pressed a finger against her lips and whispered to us that it would be best to let the patient have as much rest as possible. I apologised and said I was leaving. Celia accompanied me to the entrance of the hospital.

Celia said as she saw me out, "Why don't you go to my house and wait for me? That will be nice." She held out the keys for me even before I could nod assent.

"Okay," I said, "but don't be long."

"I won't stay any longer than necessary," she said. "But I'd like to meet with Dr Watson and watch over Mrs Feston for a while yet to see that everything's all right. You'd better make yourself comfortable at home and get yourself some rest in the meantime. You must be tired."

Chapter 18

I took a taxi to Craven Manor. It was quite late and the house was in complete darkness. It had taken more than thirty minutes to drive from the hospital, which was at the other end of town. I paid the cabbie, opened the house's large front door with the keys Celia had given me, and switched on the lights in the hall. Although the bright bulbs from the chandelier flooded the room with light, it felt eerie to be alone in the immense silence of that sprawling mansion. The furniture, although lovely, was of a bygone generation, massive in proportion and solemn in appearance, lacking the gaiety and brightness of modern design. The house felt strangely sinister as I sat there all by myself, and I couldn't help feeling a sense of foreboding.

I pulled off my coat and threw it on the settee and loosened my tie. The prominent glass cabinet, well stocked with an assortment of spirits, wines, and liqueurs, was tempting. I needed a pick-me-up and something to do. I slid the glass panel aside and pulled out a bottle of whisky and a glass. I poured a stiff drink and splashed in a squirt of soda from the siphon on the sideboard. I sat down and took a good gulp, crossed my knees, and lit my pipe. The drink warmed my insides and made me feel cosy and satisfied.

Celia, I knew, would be back in a little while. It was just like her to be so concerned about Mrs Feston; she had to meet the doctor to assure herself that all was well. Tenderness for Celia welled up within me. She was so kind and gentle, as a woman should be, yet she had an authority all her own which brooked no nonsense. As a wife should be, I thought with a smile.

The big grandfather clock against the wall chimed and startled me out of my thoughts. It struck eight, each chime echoing down the hall in a long wave. No sooner had it finished when a sudden clanging came from somewhere upstairs, which made me jump out of my seat.

"Who's there?" I called but got no reply.

It was as if a glass pane had been shattered. In a moment I had climbed the stairs and put on the corridor lights. I heaved a sigh of relief as I saw Celia's big black cat scuttle off the tea trolley that sat in the corridor opposite Celia's room. The cat had upset the silver lid of the teapot. I picked it up and replaced it on the tray. I started back down the stairs, and it struck me how steep the staircase was. Poor Mrs Feston! She was indeed lucky to have escaped with her life. The staircase was divided into two flights, each joined by a landing, and each flight contained as many as twenty steps. If she had fallen from the top of the staircase, she would have tumbled down all those steps before reaching the landing, which would have broken the momentum and prevented her from rolling farther down the second flight.

I had reached the landing when it occurred to me that I hadn't switched off the light at the top of the stairs. So I reluctantly climbed back up once more. The light at the top was quite bright and shed its beams almost down the entire length of the stairway, reflecting off the varnished steps. I paused awhile to catch my breath, as I had ascended with more than necessary gusto. I was about to take the last few steps up to the landing when my eye caught a small, freshly splintered hole in the wainscot to the left of the step before the landing. I bent over. There could be no doubt about it – the hole had been created by a nail that must have been hammered in and jerked out again. I ran my fingers along its top and a wild thought took possession of my mind. Almost in a frenzy, I looked at the other side of the step, and as I feared, there was another similar hole and a long scratch on the wood from when the nail had been jerked out.

Yes! There could not be any mistake. It was from here that Mrs Feston had fallen. Her scared look and impassioned plea that I not leave her and her statement, "I am afraid … stairs," came to mind. In a flash, the awful realisation came to me that someone had tried to murder Mrs Feston with this simple booby trap. She must have tripped across a wire or string that spanned the step and had been affixed to the nails on either side. What a simple and yet effective device to trip anyone, and with such devastating results. The shock was all too sudden; I sat down with my head in my hands and tried to think. My mind was in a whirl, and I asked myself who could have wanted to do such a terrible thing, and why.

Chapter 19

A terrifying thought crossed my mind, and in a moment I rose from my seat and sped down the stairs. I picked up my coat from the chair, opened the front door, pulled it shut behind me, and half-ran all the way down the drive and into the street. A taxi ground to a halt at my sudden frantic signalling. "To the hospital," I said, banging the door closed. "And hurry – please hurry."

"Yes, mister," the driver, an old veteran, said. He looked perplexed but rose to the occasion.

Although he did his best, he had to stop at traffic signs and pedestrian crossings, making the journey to the hospital seem to take hours although it took barely thirty minutes.

I rushed inside and wished the hospital porter good evening and requested that he allow me to see Sister Elfreda. He was a genial chap but stated that no visitors were allowed into the wards at that hour. I explained to him that it was urgent, but it was of no use.

"Sorry, guv." He smiled. "Rules is rules. You appreciate that, don't you? Why don't you visit Casualty? The doctor there might be able to help." But I knew that no doctor could help in the matter I was concerned about. There was no time to waste; rules or no rules, it just couldn't be helped.

"I'm sorry, old chap," I said brushing past the porter. "This is something that cannot wait. I'll explain later."

"Hey, mister!" I heard him shout as I fairly ran down the corridor towards Mrs Feston's room. Halfway down I nearly bumped into Sister Elfreda. I stopped, panting.

"What on earth are you doing here at this hour, Mr Benison?" she said, quite taken aback. "I thought you'd left earlier."

"I am sorry, Sister," I said. "Is Mrs Murray in? Just dropped by to see if she was still here."

"Oh, no," the Sister said, rolling her eyes. "She left about twenty minutes ago. Came and saw me in my room before going. She must be on her way home. Why, is anything the matter?"

"Nothing, er ... nothing at all," I replied. "Just ... er ... had a message for her. How is Mrs Feston?

"I expect she's asleep. I was just going to see her. Mrs Murray said she was all right."

"May I join you, Sister?" I said. "I'd like to see her before leaving."

"Well, I suppose it should be all right," Sister Elfreda said reluctantly, "but we can't be too long."

Mrs Feston seemed sound asleep, her head well propped up on the pillows. Sister Elfreda tiptoed to the bed and looked down on the patient. I followed, my heart beating wildly.

"She's asleep," Sister Elfreda whispered into my ear, but I noticed no movement of breathing. I picked up Mrs Feston's hand, which lay by her side. I could feel no pulse.

"You might wake her," Sister Elfreda cautioned.

"Nothing can wake her now," I said. "Mrs Feston, I am afraid, is dead."

"Dead?" the Sister said incredulously. "But that's impossible. Mrs Murray said only a few minutes back that she was keeping very well. Must have been sudden."

She took Mrs Feston's hand and felt for her pulse.

"How unfortunate," she said, shaking her head. "I thought she'd pull through. We didn't think her condition warranted a heart monitor. You wait here, Mr Benison. I'll alert the duty nurse."

Standing by Mrs Feston's bed, I took stock of the room. Everything was just as I had left it earlier in the evening. My eyes came to rest on the dead face of Mrs Feston. On closer scrutiny, I saw marks there of strain and suffering, and a thin trickle of saliva had oozed down the side of her mouth and dried. A lock of hair floated untidily across her forehead. My eyes turned to her pillow and my heart missed a beat at what I noticed. There was a slight damp patch on it and the edge of the pillow was crumpled. In her semi-conscious state, she could have offered only the weakest resistance. The pillow was crushed where it had been bent over.

I straightened up with a shock as I heard footsteps along the corridor, and Sister Elfreda came in accompanied by another nurse. Sister Elfreda expressed her commiseration and surprise, but I barely heard what she had to say. I had only one frenzied thought in my mind; I had to talk to Celia.

"Excuse me, Sister," I heard myself say, "may I use your telephone? I must inform Mrs Murray."

"Yes, of course," she said. "You know where my office is, don't you? Do help yourself."

I thanked her and left.

Sister Elfreda's cubicle was right down the ward. I half-ran to it and picked up the telephone and dialled Celia's number. I listened to the buzzing at the other end. My hands trembled. After what seemed an eternity, I heard the click of the telephone being taken off its rest. It was Celia.

"Yes?" Her voice was high-pitched and tense.

"Celia," I began, "Ben, here. I am speaking from the hospital. Mrs Feston is dead."

"But that cannot be," she said. "She seemed quite well when I left her only a little more than half an hour back. What on earth made you go to the hospital?"

"I dropped in to see you," I said. "I'll be right with you in a few minutes. There is something I must ask you."

"Ben," her voice barely came through, "is everything all right? There's nothing the matter, is there?"

"No nothing at all," I said, and then in desperation, my voice choking in my throat, "but why did you have to do it? Oh! My God, why?"

"What do you mean, Ben?" Celia said, her voice an incredulous whisper.

"You know what I mean, Celia. Mrs Feston's fall down the stairs was no accident. There are nail marks on the landing that show clearly that she was deliberately tripped. Neither was her death an accident. I am at my wit's end, Celia. Please wait. I shall come at once so that we can talk about all this."

I heard a gasp from Celia, but not waiting to hear her reply, I put down the receiver.

I was coming out of Sister Elfreda's cubicle when she accosted me. "Ah, Mr Murray," she said, "how foolish of me to have forgotten. There was a note for you from Sister Julia, who was on duty last evening. Dear me, I am sorry I forgot to give it to you earlier this evening. It is in my diary in the office."

She walked past me into the cubicle and picked up a small black diary from the table. She plucked out a folded piece of paper sticking out from between the pages and handed it to me.

"Sister Julia tells me that Mrs Feston seemed overwrought and insisted on calling for you. She seemed terribly upset and frightened and requested that this message be given only to you. She was in a semi-coma, poor thing! It's something about a car – quite unintelligible, it seems to me."

I took the note from the Sister, my curiosity aroused, and my mind numb with a queer sense of expectancy.

"Well, I must be going, and so must you, I'm afraid," Sister Elfreda said briskly and left. I opened the note and read it.

> Dear Mr Benison,
>
> Sometime last evening Mrs Feston had a brief spell of consciousness and seemed anxious that she should see you. I told her that that would not be possible until the next day, since it was late in the evening. She then insisted that I inform you as follows: What she had wanted to tell you when you last spoke was that there had been nothing wrong with Celia's car, which she had used that day, and that she had been asked not to mention it to you or anyone. She said you would understand. She also said she was scared and wanted to see you very urgently. She was very weak, and her mind wandered, but she seemed quite in possession of her faculties at the time of giving this message. I tried to ask her what she meant, but she said you would understand.
>
> Sister Julia

Now it struck me that this was what Mrs Feston had been trying to tell me the last time I had spoken to her at Craven Manor, before our conversation was interrupted by Celia's return from the shops. So this was the information that Celia had asked her not to divulge to me.

Chapter 20

Mrs Feston's revelation kept revolving in my mind as I hastened from the hospital and called for a taxi. What on earth had she been trying to convey to me? I wondered if her words had been the mere unintelligible ramblings of a mind delirious with fever and pain. And yet her reference to the secret which she had intended to tell me showed that her utterances seemed to be sensible. And then I recalled what Celia had told me on the day I had gone over and talked to Miss Polycarpou, namely, that she could not give me a lift home because her car was inoperable. She had also, thereafter, visited the garage with me to request that a mechanic repair the car. So what could Mrs Feston have meant by saying that there had been nothing wrong with the car and that she had actually driven it?

I felt helplessly perplexed, my mind pervaded by a sense of doom. As the taxi approached Craven Manor, my heart beat uncontrollably. I was overwhelmed and quite put out at the prospect of meeting Celia. I had so much to ask her, but I felt apprehensive.

I knew I should inform the Chief Inspector of the situation immediately, but I could not resist the urge to meet Celia one last time.

As we entered the drive, I could see the lights on in the hall. As the taxi swung towards the porch, its headlights focussed for a moment on the garage. As I had feared, it was empty; Celia had taken the car out. And then the entire meaning of what Mrs Feston had tried to tell me struck me with sudden clarity. Yes, there had been nothing wrong with Celia's car, and that was the secret that Mrs Feston had tried to convey. And this meant, of course, that Celia had deliberately lied; her story that she was unable to use the car was a charade. But why had she lied?

My mind now was saturated with suspicion. I asked the driver to wait, climbed up the steps leading to the front door, and tried the handle. It was locked. Having knocked and got no answer, I inserted the spare key Celia had given me and opened the door. I was in a dither as to what to do next when I noticed an envelope directly under the light on the dining table. Instinctively I knew it must be for me. I stepped across the hall and picked it up. My name was written on it in Celia's hand. Hastily, my fingers taut and trembling, I opened the envelope and drew out the neatly folded note. Overcome with nervous exhaustion I slumped into a chair and read it. The handwriting was large and scrawling, as if written in great haste.

My dearest Ben,

>Please forgive me for running away like this, but I know that it is no use. I couldn't face you now and answer your questions, and I am too weary to lie to you.
>
>I am sorry, very sorry, that it had to be you who found me out. Isn't it so ridiculously ironical, Ben, that you – who were my one source of strength and security – should be the one to discover the skeleton in my cupboard and blow up everything to fragments?
>
>I know you love me, Ben, but I also know that you could never condone what I have done, so I must take the only course open to me.
>
>But first, I must tell you what you probably suspect. You've seen the marks on the staircase and you know I killed Mrs Feston. But I had to. You will see why.
>
>I must tell you also, since it no longer matters, that I also killed Don. Does that surprise you? You see, Ben, I loved Don so terribly and I always told him that I would kill him if he ever was unfaithful to me.
>
>That evening when you went to meet Don, I had already planned it all out. I knew that if I drove fast, I could, with luck, be in the vicinity of the Clarendon in time to see you arrive. Mrs Feston was away. I lied about the state of my car.

I made you promise not to tell Don about that evening because I wanted to catch him off guard. When I reached London, it was around seven. I parked my car in one of the alleys along Oxford Street near Marble Arch and watched the hotel. You arrived about fifteen minutes later, and I saw Don open the door for you. You were with him for perhaps forty minutes, and then you came out and left. I waited for about ten minutes before dropping in on Don. I opened the door with the key he kept on the doorsill. He had such a shock, but I pretended that I had come to surprise him with a visit. I must thank you for having kept your word, for he didn't suspect that I knew anything.

When I saw him, I felt terribly repulsed by his deceit. Villain, smiling villain – oh, how I hated him! I introduced a sleeping draught into Don's whisky, which I had no difficulty inveigling him to take, it being his usual practice at that hour. I declined one myself on the grounds of an upset stomach. The sleeping pills – two, to be exact, which I had crushed in advance into powder – I had obtained about six months before from Uncle John Haversham on one of my weekend visits, when he over-solicitously foisted them on me because I had had mild insomnia. I had not used them but carried them back with me to Wimbledon, where I kept them just in case. After Don had gulped down his drink in his usual fashion and complained of not feeling well, I got him into bed. He was soon snoring away, and I turned on the gas tap, closed the door, and left. I was sure the gas would finish him off quickly, as the tap was only a few feet from the bedhead.

Next, I walked down to my car, but after I was halfway down the drive, it suddenly occurred to me that I must have left one of my gloves in Don's room. I re-parked my car and hastened back, opened Don's door with the key I had earlier replaced on the doorsill, and entered Don's room. The room was fairly reeking by then with the smell of gas. I found the glove on the dining table and, covering my nose with it, checked Don's pulse. He was dead. The gas was already beginning to suffocate, so I closed the tap and left the room. Closing the gas tap, of course, was a terrible mistake, since my plan was to make it look like suicide. But by the time this dawned on me, I was already on my way to Wimbledon and I couldn't bring myself to go back.

Of course, you will realise it was I Mrs Blaine had seen coming out of Don's room with the glove to my nose. It turned out, however, that she had also seen Ada Hamilton briefly enter and leave Don's room at around the same time. So, when Mrs Blaine saw in the newspapers the news of Don's death and the suspected foul play, she put two and two together and surmised that it was I who had been responsible. The situation was ideal from her point of view because everyone suspected Miss Hamilton. She decided to take advantage of the situation – to conceal her knowledge of my visit, to falsely implicate Miss Hamilton, and to blackmail me for the sum of £10,000, which I agreed to pay.

I reached Wimbledon around 10.30 p.m. and a further shock awaited me. The lights on the staircase came on and Mrs Feston appeared. I had not expected her back until the next day, but she said that she had decided to come back earlier. She said that she had heard the car being parked and wanted to know where I'd been. I don't know what came over me then – I panicked. I made her promise not to mention to anyone that I had left home, as it wouldn't look nice for me since I had refused you a lift on grounds that my car was out of order, although, really, I was too tired and upset to drop you off. This explanation seemed to satisfy her.

In order to take all suspicion away from my having used the car, I loosened the battery terminals and replaced a working fuse with a burnt-out one I had in the garage from a previous repair.

You will see why it was necessary that I should kill Mrs Feston. I thought she would keep her promise, but I had an inkling that she would tell you about it sooner or later. When I came in from my shopping I overheard her telling you something about the car. I was at first afraid that she may have already told you, but you did not give any indication that she had. If the police came to know that I had been away from the house, my alibi would have been blown, and they may have investigated my movements.

So, my dearest, there you have it all. I have no regrets except that we could have got on so well together. Anyway, it's goodbye now. Yes, I know I have no other choice but to take my own life. And somehow I feel it is such a relief to know that it will all be over soon – all the fear and the wretchedness and this terrible turbulence within me.

Goodbye, dearest,

Celia.

I put the letter down. My whole body seemed weighed down, and my limbs felt numb and lifeless. Inside me I felt an ineffable sadness, an irrevocable loss, and an aching despair. My feelings for Celia were tinged with pity and yes – love. Poor Celia. She had so much wanted to be loved that it was the end of her whole world when Don had betrayed her. I thought how curious it was that Celia, who had been such an ideal wife and a kind and gentle human being so long as she had the security of her husband's love, should become the perverse murderess that she had become. Deep down in my heart I knew, of course, that she had to be sick, so terribly sick, to have become what she had. I was aghast at what she had done. She had, of course, been right – I naturally could never have condoned her actions. It suddenly occurred to me that she might have had a way out if she had decided to dispose of me as well. I no longer had any illusions that she would have done so if she could. I was sure the thought must have crossed her mind, but then she had reached a point where her mind could not take any more and the prospect of suicide became the only attractive way out.

Chapter 21

There was a knock at the door. I remembered that the taxi driver was still waiting for me. I opened the door for him.

"Will you be long then, guv?" he asked, his toothless, wrinkled face peering up at me.

I folded Celia's letter, placed it inside my coat pocket, and stepped into the taxi.

My mind raced, but all my thoughts ended in blind alleys. It was impossible to tell where Celia had gone and what exactly she was planning to do – what gruesome scheme she was going to employ to kill herself. I decided that the only avenue open was to go to the police.

"Where to, guv?" the driver asked for the second time.

"The police station," I said, "and hurry, please."

I sat on the edge of my seat, my hands gripping the back of the seat in front of me, my heart racing with impatience. One part of me was desperate at the thought of Celia taking her life and frantic to stop her doing so, whilst my better judgment told me that there was no use trying to stop her – it would be best that way. There was nothing anybody could do to help Celia. There would be no mercy for her.

When we reached the police station, there were only a duty sergeant at his post and a young constable in one of the offices making entries in a diary. A police jeep, probably returning from a night patrol, parked noisily under the front porch. I had told the taxi driver to wait and was still in a daze as I approached the duty sergeant's desk.

The man appeared to recognise me, although I could not recall having seen him before, and he addressed me before I had the opportunity to open my mouth.

"Good evening, sir," he said. "You are Mr Benison, aren't you? Can I be of service to you, sir?"

"Yes, Sergeant," I said. "I, er, came to report a missing person. I mean, I believe a lady I know may … need help."

"I beg your pardon, sir?" the Sergeant said. His eyes were wide like an owl's and his mouth half-open. I must have cut quite an odd figure and sounded quite unintelligible.

It was quite hopeless. What sort of statement could I possibly make? It seemed ridiculous to tell the Sergeant that I had received a letter that indicated that the writer planned to take her own life. What were the police supposed to do?

My mind worked frantically to think of what Celia would do if, indeed, she planned to end her life. My thoughts flashed back to our conversation of a few nights back as we drove over the railway tracks after our dinner at the Café Royale. She had made reference to *Anna Karenina* and the heroine throwing herself in the way of a train. Instinctively, I knew that was where Celia would go and that was what she too planned to do.

"I must stop her!" I said loudly to myself. The Sergeant looked thoroughly puzzled, and I hastened out of the building. I ran to the taxi, climbed in, and slammed the door. I gave directions to the driver, adding, "And hurry, please. It's a matter of life or death."

The taxi driver jerked the car forwards. In about ten minutes, we came in sight of the bridge, and my heart plummeted as I discerned a frail figure wrapped in an overcoat silhouetted against the skyline by the moonlight. It was unmistakably Celia, and I inwardly thanked God that I was in time to stop her.

"Hurry, please hurry!" I cried, leaning forward in my seat as we turned towards the bridge. There Celia stood, swaying as if blown by the wind, her hands on the iron barrier, her body leaning forwards. I felt a surge of hope that I would be able to gather her in my arms and save her. But as the car climbed to the bridge, I heard the distinct sound of an approaching train and the loud, clear hoot of its horn. In the next moment there was a puff of smoke to the left of the bridge, and in an instant, as the train sped towards the tunnel, Celia's figure plunged onto the track below.

By the time we reached the bridge, the train had disappeared around a bend in the track. My eyes searched frantically for any evidence of Celia. In the dim light of the moon, the track was not clearly visible, but it would still have been possible to discern a body. It did not, of course, occur to my frenzied mind that if Celia's body had been hurled into the path of an oncoming train it would, in all probability, have been pitchforked away from the track by the impact. In any case, I saw nothing beyond the area immediately bordering the track, as the land on either side of it sloped away into woodland.

"Can you see anything?" I asked the cabbie, who had joined me.

"Not a thing, guv," he said matter-of-factly. "I bet she must have been done in. Better we report the matter to the police so they can send a search party. I'm sorry. Guess she was someone close to you?"

I nodded, and he said again that he was sorry. The shock had left me dazed and filled with grief. I went back to the taxi, and we drove to the police station. The Sergeant I had earlier spoken to was still behind his desk. I reported the incident, and the cabbie confirmed it. I urged that the police investigate the incident immediately in case Celia was somehow still alive and that the Sergeant give orders for a patrol to go to the scene. The Sergeant asked if I wished to accompany them, but I didn't think I could face discovering Celia's mangled body. I told him I was very upset and tired and needed to take a rest.

I bade him goodnight and asked the taxi driver to take me home.

Chapter 22

I was awakened by insistent knocking on my door. It was Tomlinson.

"I am sorry to have awakened you, sir, but a Sergeant Bates from the Wimbledon police is here to see you. He says it's very urgent."

I looked at my watch. It was one thirty a.m. That explained why Tomlinson had to make such a din to get me up. The shock of the previous evening's ordeal had certainly lulled me into a deep sleep.

"Thank you, Tom," I said, jumping out of bed, now fully awake. "Please tell the Sergeant I will be down in a minute."

I hastened to the toilet propelled by the memory of what had transpired only a few hours before, terribly anxious to know what news the Sergeant had concerning Celia. With a sinking feeling in my stomach and my heart beating audibly in my breast, I ran through my ablutions like a man demented, dressed in great haste, and was down in a trice.

"Good morning, Sergeant," I said as I caught sight of him in the hall. "Have you any news of Mrs Murray?"

Sergeant Bates rose to his feet awkwardly, fidgeting with a handkerchief in his hands. He was a small-boned man whom I immediately recognised as the person who had visited Celia's on the night of Don's death in the company of Inspector Hargreaves.

"I am afraid I do, sir," he said. "Sorry to disturb you so early in the morning, but we thought you'd want to know. It is very bad news indeed. The search party found her dead body, which had been thrown by the train about twenty yards from the scene of the accident."

"Oh my God," I said, pressing the palm of my hand to my forehead. "Was death instantaneous?"

"Oh yes, sir," said the Sergeant. "There could be no doubt about that."

"In what condition was her body recovered?" I asked.

The Sergeant explained that the body had been very badly mangled and that one of her limbs had been severed. He requested that I come down to the police station later that morning to identify Celia's body at the mortuary. I agreed to do so.

Sergeant Bates had barely left when the phone rang. It was Chief Inspector Smith calling from London.

"I am truly sorry," he said, "to hear of Mrs Murray's death. Inspect Hargreaves told me there has been a terrible accident.

I understand that you indicated to the police that it may have been suicide. Is that correct?"

I confirmed to him that it was so. I also told him of Celia's letter and of her confession of Don's murder.

The Chief Inspector was truly shocked. "Oh my. This makes us look bloody fools, doesn't it? We initially had Mrs Murray on our list of likely suspects and even had a man assigned, as a matter of routine, to trail her movements, but we found nothing to implicate her even remotely in Mr Murray's murder. And to think that our case against Miss Hamilton was so strong as to almost certainly have convicted her of the murder! What a cock-up!"

I mumbled something about meeting the Chief Inspector some time that week, bade him goodbye, and put down the receiver.

I felt emotionally spent, hollow, and hopeless, combined with an aching despair. I had loved Celia dearly, but it was not destined that we should be together. I had lost her once to Don, and now, forever, just as I was beginning to reclaim her love. This grief would haunt me all my life, would leave an indelible mark on everything I was to do and be. I tried to hold back the welling tears as I walked slowly and heavily up the dimly lit stairs into the beckoning darkness of my room.

www.ingramcontent.com/pod-product-compliance
Lightning Source LLC
LaVergne TN
LVHW091546060526
838200LV00036B/726